# SEG THE BOWMAN

Seg the Bowman is the story, complete in itself, of the finest
archer of two worlds, a man courageous and resolute in the
face of adversity, a wild, fey, reckless fellow, blade comrade
to Dray Prescot, a man of parts. Of Seg Segutorio it has been
said that perhaps he is too kind-hearted for the harsher aspects
of the world of Kregen.

Kregen, a planet orbiting Antares four hundred light years
from Earth, is indeed a harsh world; but it is also beautiful
and mysterious, exotic and immensely rewarding, where many
a dream may be realized, many a nightmare become reality.

The story begins where Seg and Dray Prescot and a party
of adventurers have successfully quitted a maze of monsters
and sorcery. Prescot is called away by the Star Lords as
related in *Fires of Scorpio*. Now Seg steps forward into fresh
adventures wherein he discovers the passionate problems of
agreeing to act as the lady Milsi's knightly protector.

The warmth and pride suffusing Dray Prescot's words as
he tells the story of Seg Segutorio confirm the powerful
friendship between the two and illuminates their mutual loyalty.
For they are blade comrades upon the haunting world of
Kregen beneath the streaming mingled radiance of the Suns
of Scorpio.

*Alan Burt Akers*

The adventures of Dray Prescot
are narrated in DAW Books:

# SEG
# THE
# BOWMAN

by
**Dray Prescot**

As told to
Alan Burt Akers

**DAW Books, Inc.**
Donald A. Wollheim, Publisher
1633 Broadway, New York, N.Y. 10019

PUBLISHED BY
THE NEW AMERICAN LIBRARY
OF CANADA LIMITED

Daw Collectors' Book Number 598

First Printing, October 1984

2  3  4  5  6  7  8  9

 DAW TRADEMARK REGISTERED
U.S. PAT. OFF. MARCA REGISTRADA.
HECHO EN WINNIPEG, CANADA

PRINTED IN CANADA
COVER PRINTED IN U.S.A.

# TABLE OF CONTENTS

# CHAPTER ONE

## Phantom of the Jungle

The woman in the blue tunic halted just inside the edge of the jungle and, shading her eyes against the twin suns, stared out toward the lake. The two men walking toward her might be deep in conversation; she knew well enough even in the short time she had made their acquaintance that if she moved another step they would see her at once.

A vague blue haze pulsed unexpectedly about the men, making her blink her eyes. She did not move. The twin suns threw down their mingled streaming lights and in the early morning radiance shadows still stretched short into emerald and ruby blobs. The strange blueness appeared to swish into her eyes like the bewildering swirl of a dancer's cape.

When she looked out again there was only one man on the little path by the lake.

Alarmed, she called out.

"Seg the Horkandur!"

At the sound of his name the man looked up

instantly. He was in the act of picking up from the
path a length of scarlet cloth and a longsword.
From these two items he drew his attention not so
much reluctantly as regretfully. He faced the
woman.

"Yes, my lady?"

"Is all—is all well? Where is the Bogandur?"

"He has been—called away."

She laughed uncertainly. "Called away? Here in
the midst of this terrible jungle?"

"Do not fret over him, my lady. He will turn up
in his own good time."

"Yes, I believe that. For I thought him dead
back there in that horrendous mountain."

"As did I. He was not an apparition, I assure
you. Stand very still, my lady. When I shout run,
run!"

The scarlet breechclout and the longsword went
thump onto the path. The longbow snapped into
Seg's left hand, the shaft was nocked and the
string drawn in a blur of speed. The first arrow
sped.

That shaft passed a scant hand's breadth past the
woman's ear. Seg bellowed as he loosed.

"Run, my Lady Milsi, run!"

Milsi ran.

A gargantuan screech burst out from the jungle
just to her rear. A bellow and a thrashing of
densely packed foliage drove her on, panting with
effort. A second arrow flew, and a third followed
on while the second was still in the air.

Milsi panted down out of the jungle edge, pursued by what horrors she did not know. But she
had complete confidence in Seg the Horkandur.
She had known him for so short a time, yet he had

proved to be the perfect jikai, the honorable warrior, devoted to her person.

With the same blurring speed Seg thrust the bow stave up over his left shoulder and whipped out his sword.

Yelling in a deliberate attempt to engage the monster's attention, he drove forward venomously.

The sword flamed in his fist.

He roared past Milsi without a glance, a word. Every instinct of his body concentrated on the slavering thing lashing about by the jungle edge. The three shafts had done their work. For Seg, a Bowman of Loh, anything else would have smacked of the impossible in any world, ordered or not. He brought the sword down and around and hacked a gouting chunk from the beast's neck. One eye remained, a glaring orb of hatred. That eye blacked into a gush of ichor as the sword punched in.

Seg leaped back.

The thing, scaled and vicious, lashed about in its death throes. As long as a man, it reared up on six legs to waist height. Its head, sharp with jaws and teeth, twisted from side to side. Twice it reached up on its four hind legs, the front claws slicing at empty air.

A voice bellowed from farther into the forest.

"Hai!"

The scaled beast attempted to turn itself around, and weakened by loss of blood, fell. It toppled into the scrubby undergrowth by the side of the trail. It thrashed about. And then it died.

Seg gave it a last calculating look, and turned and ran back to Milsi.

"You are unharmed, Seg?"

"Aye. By the Veiled Froyvil! I am glad you came to no harm."

"Thanks only to you. I give you the jikai."

"Aye," bellowed the voice as its owner pounded out into the clearing. "Hai, Jikai!"

Seg ignored all that. It was not a jikai in his estimation. We'd shafted the poor thing thrice, and then chopped it a trifle. A mere nothing before breakfast for a warrior upon the world of Kregen.

"What is it, anyway?"

"That is a toilca—"

"Well, Hop, it is dead now."

"Maybe." Hop the Intemperate spoke through the mass of hair about his mouth, his gross body as hairy through his harness as a quoffa. "But they do not hunt singly. They wander in packs."

Seg looked at the toilca, seeing the way the scales were patterned in brown and green to give superb camouflage. The shape was adapted to slinking through the jungle, and when the toilcas surrounded their victim, they would rear up on their hind legs and tear the poor devil to pieces with their front claws.

"In that case, friend Hop, we had best get back to the others sharpish."

"I'm with you, Horkandur. Master Exandu sent me to follow the Lady Milsi. He complained that she wandered off into the jungle like a—" Here Hop the Intemperate belied his name, for he stopped talking at that point.

Quite clearly Exandu had passed uncomplimentary comments about a woman wandering off into the jungle like a loon.

The Lady Milsi fired up.

"I could not sleep. I was worried about where Seg the Horkandur had gone, so I followed—"

"Let us go back to the others," interrupted Seg. "But, first. . . ."

He ran back down the path and snatched up the scarlet breechclout and the longsword. When he got back to Milsi and Hop, the latter said: "They belong to the Bogandur! I thought the demon ate him."

"So did I. But he has had to go off—"

"A mighty strange fellow, that. More strange even than you, Horkandur!"

Seg made no reply to this, for he agreed. Maintaining a close watch upon the forest, they walked back along the rudimentary trail to the clearing where the party were rousing out after the night's uneasy sleep. The smell of the first breakfast filled the air with mouth-watering aromas.

Looking at the Lady Milsi as she swung along, Seg reflected that she was, in Erthyr's very truth, a wonderful person. Her body, firm and voluptuous, filled the blue tunic. Her face glowed with the remembered horrors through which they had passed to arrive here, and of which that poor toilca had been but merely the latest. She had managed to wash her hair in the last of the chambers in the mountain where the party had rested and eaten before at last quitting the abode of horrors. Her hair was of a bright and sheening brown, and the dinginess and stringiness were gone. She held herself proudly. Well, and so she should, seeing that she was a lady in waiting to a queen—well, poor Queen Mab was dead now. He and his comrade had taken the Lady Milsi from the next cell.

And that made Seg wonder where the devil his

old dom might be now. Anywhere on Kregen, perhaps been spirited back to that funny little world he'd spoken of, called Earth, a long long way away, where they only had one little yellow sun and one little silver moon, and only had apims like him, instead of the multifarious and wonderful assemblage of diffs inhabiting Kregen.

"You look—severe, Seg."

"It is nothing, my lady. I but thought of the Bogandur. I wish him well. But now we must look to ourselves and get out of this pestiferous jungle."

"Yes. But where to?"

He looked surprised.

"Why—surely you will wish to return home? Of course, I shall escort you. That is, if you wish it."

"You know I wish it. . . ."

"So that is settled."

"I hope so. It may not be so—so easy as all that."

Seg sniffed and put on an air of long-suffering. He was not the kind of fellow to allow himself to be down in the dumps for too long.

For her part, Milsi looked at Seg and saw a man endowed with superlative attributes. He possessed the archer's build, broad of shoulder, trim of waist, with the muscles like live snakes upon his bronzed body. He wore a scarlet breechclout, cinctured by a broad lesten hide belt. He carried his Lohvian longbow, and the quiver of arrows, each fletched with rose-red feathers. His sword was of a pattern with which she was not familiar. His moccasins, like hers, were supple of uppers and stout of sole. The party had worn through a good many pairs of those arriving here, and were like to wear through a lot more before they escaped this place.

These surface attributes were apparent to other people as well as to Seg and Milsi when they looked one upon the other. But each saw more than the surface. Each saw in the other a spark of life, a steady sureness of purpose, loyalty, cheerfulness, a sense that each yearned for targets that more mundane folk might consider eternally out of reach.

Seg had sworn to be Milsi's jikai, and to care for her and escort her. For her part, she had promised him nothing. They had met in the maze of the mountain when the party sought bandit treasure, and Milsi had been rescued. Her party, led by the queen in search of the king, were all dead. Now, Seg realized, she would have to return and report that fact.

For some people the fact would not be sad. For some of the schemers the news would brighten up their day. . . .

Although Milsi had said nothing to make him think he stood more highly in her affections than anyone else, he felt confident she regarded him with approval as her escort.

That was a start.

He sniffed the breakfast scents approvingly.

Milsi glanced up at him as Hop hurried forward toward the bulky and complaining figure of Master Exandu.

"It is odd, Seg. You say you are from Loh. Of course, I know nothing of that continent; but I have heard that all Lohvians have red hair—"

He laughed, his fey blue eyes very merry.

"Come and have something to eat! No, no. I come from Erthyrdrin, which is in the very north of Loh. Up there we mostly have black hair and blue eyes. There are red-headed folk among us—and I can tell you, we make jokes about that!"

"I'm sure."

"What!" yelped Exandu. He spluttered, tottering. "This is terrible! We must move on at once, get away from this fearful place—oh, my insides. Shanli! Shanli! My insides burn—it is that infernal vosk rasher I have just eaten. . . . Shanli, for the sweet sake of Beng Sbodine, the Mender of Men!"

Clearly, Hop the Intemperate had just told Exandu that a crazed pack of toilcas was on the loose and threatening to rush headlong upon the camp and devour everyone about the fires.

Shanli hurried up in her graceful fashion of not seeming to fuss or hurry at all but of always being on hand to fetch Exandu a sip of wine, a potion, liniment, and most importantly of all soothing words.

"A potion of Mother Babli's Stomach Balm, master. And I have mixed it with just a sip of Honeyed Jholaix."

"Oh, Shanli, my treasure. . . . Honeyed Jholaix!"

Seg noticed the way Milsi reacted to this pathetic tomfoolery. Her eyebrows rose. Yet, she was well aware of the parlous state of Exandu's insides, and of his interminable lamentations about his liver, and bones, and aching head.

She saw Seg looking at her.

"Honeyed Jholaix, indeed! That is pure decadence."

Jholaix, being the name of the country and of its wines, the finest, so folk swore, in this part of

Kregen, was well known as a wine and not often sampled. A poor man could not afford to buy a prime bottle of Jholaix with a year's wages.

"Yes, but, lady Milsi," said Shanli with her deep and resigned manner giving her a transcendental appearance of purity—"Master Exandu deserves all and more anyone can offer—"

"I'm sure."

"Toilcas!" burst out Exandu, taking a heartbeat to chatter around the cup Shanli held to his shaking lips.

"They shall not harm you, master, not with Hop the Intemperate and Seg the Horkandur and all the other fine guards with us."

Seg caught the eye of the Pachak, Kalu Na-Fre. Kalu walked over carrying a morning cup of tea in his tail hand, his upper left hand holding an enormous slice of bread, his lower left hand a pot of preserves. His single right hand dipped a knife into the pot and smeared the golden-yellow preserve upon the bread. He wore his full harness and carried an assortment of weapons. Even taking breakfast upon Kregen, especially in a Kregan jungle, a fellow did not wander about defenseless.

"Toilcas?" He sounded pleased.

"Aye. And, Kalu, you and I know that Exandu here will swing his sword lustily enough if the time comes."

"Do you not think, masters," put in Shanli, still spooning the potion into Exandu, "that we should pack up and depart at once?"

"The question is one upon which a fine argument might be built," observed Kalu the Pachak. His straw-yellow hair swirled as he turned to regard Shanli. Short, Pachaks stood in general, but fierce and ferocious warriors with one of the strongest honor codes in all the world.

"Argument, argument?" cried Master Exandu. He was a man who enjoyed the good things of life. Normally his face was rubicund and merry, with fat scarlet cheeks and eyes almost hidden in cheerful folds of flesh. And his nose! Ripe, protuberant, of a size awesome and a color glowing like the finest plumtree fruit. "There is no argument. We must leave before the monsters are upon us and devour us limb from limb."

"Oh," said Kalu, casually. "I believe they're more inclined to swallow you whole, and make you last a whole sennight. Although," and in his Pachak way he looked meaningfully at Exandu. "Although, Master Exandu, they might make you last a pair of weeks; they'd not take you down whole."

Mistress Shanli decided that her poor dear master could stand no more of this, and she urged him off between the campfires to a resting place more seemly. She was not slave, for the comb in her long dark hair glittered, and although, like the others in the party, she had been at pain to strip away her old clothes and contrive fresh, she still wore her bronze-link belt.

There were six principals in this party adventuring after treasure in the mountain of the Coup Blag. Each principal took along his retainers, all except Seg, who had now lost his comrade.

The sixth member of the party, Skort the Clawsang, had been lost within the depths of the maze in the mountain. Now Fregeff, the Fristle Sorcerer, walked calmly across to Kalu, Seg and the Lady Milsi.

"Toilcas are merely corporeal," said the catman in his hissing way. He brushed his whiskers with the bronzen links of his flail. Fregeff was an Adept of the Doxology of San Destinakon. The lozenges of brown and black patterning his gown bewildered the ordinary eye with their subtle shifts of alignment, suggesting awful superstitious fears to believers. The bronze chain about his waist led up to the necklet of the small winged reptile that perched upon the peak of his left shoulder. Now Fregeff put up a hand and stroked the volschrin.

"And, also, my Rik Razortooth would tear out their eyes—as you know."

Hop, about to follow Exandu, said in his bluff way: "We do know, San Fregeff. But the monsters hunt in packs. There will be many of them."

"And if I shake my bronzen flail at them?"

Hop shivered.

"That is not for mere mortal man to say, master."

The hissing sound from the catman might have been a laugh of satisfaction, if anyone there believed the sorcerer could take satisfaction from so small a point.

"All the same . . ." said Seg, and looked around. A man of parts, this strange wild archer from Erthyrdrin, and a gallant man in important matters. "Mayhap we had best move on smartly. If not for poor old Exandu's sake then for the sake of the ladies and the slaves."

The Lady Milsi's beautiful eyebrows convoluted themselves again at this. "Ladies, Seg—commingled with slaves?"

Seg remained quite unabashed,

"Certainly. I lump them together because they are unable to defend themselves—"

"Seg the Horkandur!" Now Milsi really looked annoyed. "A woman is perfectly capable of taking on and beating a craggy idiot of a man any day—"

"Some women, some men, and some days," said Seg. He spoke gently.

"Your point admits of further extension to its basic parameters," said Kalu, twitching up his tail hand but pausing to speak before he drank. "All the same, I am of the same opinion as Seg."

"Good, Kalu. I wonder if we will receive the usual tiresome contrariness from Strom Ornol?"

"Here," said Fregeff, with an indicatory jerk of his flail that did not stir the bronzen links, "he comes now."

A strom, although a little below the middle of the table of precedence, was still a rank of the higher nobility. Stroms were folk of consequence. This Strom Ornol never forgot that fact, and made sure that those around him were not forgetful, either.

The catman moved a few paces away, a small and apparently meaningless movement; but Seg was well aware that the sorcerer by that gesture was indicating that he wished to take no part in the inevitable quarrel Strom Ornol would bring with him. Fregeff as an Adept of San Destinakon was quite capable of taking care of himself in unpleasant circumstances, and it seemed that here and now the onrush of a pack of maddened toilcas was not an occurrence to make him worry overmuch. Let, he seemed to be saying, let you lesser mortals decide for the best for yourselves.

Strom Ornol, pale-faced as always, high of temper, a blot in the eyes of others beside Seg, came striding up in his usual furious temper.

"What is all this blathering? Toilcas? Who says so?"

Seg had really just about had enough of this insufferable young dandy. He knew that Ornol, as a younger son, had been kicked out by his noble father. He'd been into mischief from the day he could toddle, more than likely. Because he was a lord, Ornol had assumed that he was in command of the expedition. Seg had acquiesced in that. It went down well or ill with the other members; but only now and again had they shown open revolt. After all, they were equal members in the treasure hunting party.

"Well? Am I to receive no answer?"

Ornol fidgeted with the hilt of his rapier. The matching left-hand dagger swung over his right hip. This fashion of using rapier and main gauche was still new in the island of Pandahem, although well established in other parts of Kregen. Now Ornol glared about, his face with its pallid sheen of sweat working as though he had constipation.

"I saw one," said the Lady Milsi.

Seg said, very quickly: "Yes, pantor, that is correct."

He glanced at Milsi. She returned his look, and then glanced away. She sometimes forgot that one addressed lords properly, and here in Pandahem called them pantor, lord.

Kalu spoke up. "Well, strom. We have taken some treasure out of the mountain and are still here and alive. Unless you intend to return we may begin our return journey in all honor."

"Return? Into that hellhole?"

"That's settled, then," said Seg. He made it brisk. "Let us pack up and move out."

"I shall give the orders," started Strom Ornol.

Fregeff called in his hissing catman way: "Evil approaches."

Everybody jumped.

The Fristle sorcerer had powers, that was undeniable. If he said evil was on the way—evil was on the way.

They all looked about, and hands gripped onto sword hilts, and Seg slid his great bow off his shoulder.

"There!" yelped a Gon guard, and in the same instant they all saw the apparition floating in over the tops of the trees.

A thronelike chair hung unsupported in thin air. Its outlines were not clearly defined; it shimmered with power drawn from a source far beyond the confines of the normal. Seg blinked. He could make out the throne and the trailing silks that did not blow in the wind of the chair's passage, he could see the chavonth pelts and ling furs scattered luxuriously upon the seat and the arms, see the mantling canopy rearing out above the throne. That canopy was fashioned into the likeness of a dinosaur's wedge-shaped head, jaws agape, fangs glittering silver. The eyes were hooded ruby lights. Anyone approaching the throne must perforce stand in awe and terror of that demoniacal head above.

And—all these awesome appurtenances were as nothing beside the woman who sat on the throne.

Clad in black and green, picked out in gold, with much ornamentation and embroidery, she sat stiffly erect. Her pallor of countenance made Strom Ornol look as flushed as Master Exandu. Her eyes were green, sliding luminous slits of jade. Her hair, dark, swept in long black tresses about her shoulders and descended into a widow's peak over her forehead. She wore a jeweled band about that sleek black hair, and a smaller representation of the horrific dinosaur wedge-shaped head jutted from the center.

A guard lifted his bow. He was a Brokelsh, a member of that race of diffs who are coarse of body hair and coarse of manner. He loosed. Everyone saw. The arrow struck cleanly into the woman's breast. It passed on, transfixing that glowing phantasm, shot on and curved out and down to plunge into the jungle.

Somebody screamed.

As though nothing had happened the woman peered down from her throne. Her mouth was painted into a ripe bud shape of invitation. There was not a single line or crease upon that pallid countenance. Gold leaf decorated her eyelids. She looked down upon the mortals below.

Each one felt the force of her gaze pass over, a psychic probe, questing and passing on.

Fregeff the sorcerer stood supremely still. His bronzed flail did not quiver.

With a gesture that even in so simple a movement was all seduction, the woman lifted her left hand. Diamonds glittered. She made a sign, her forefinger pointed down at the camp in the clearing.

Among them all, Seg devoutly believed that lightning, fire and destruction would pour from that condemning finger.

Instead, the apparition wavered, the outlines flowed like gold within the smelting pot. The throne lifted away, turned, vanished beyond the tops of the trees.

In the next instant a horde of flying creatures swept out over the trees, the men astride them brandishing weapons. In an avalanche of fury, the flying warriors swept down upon the camp, lusting for the kill.

# CHAPTER TWO

## Seg the Horkandur collects arrows

Seg's instincts clashed.

His first instinct was to loose as many shafts as he could, skewer a clump of these damned flyers, and then rip out his sword and go plunging into the fight.

But, also, his first instinct was to grasp the Lady Milsi about the waist and, honoring his sworn promise to protect her, hurry her into the problematical safety of the jungle.

He could follow either course.

Where lay the course of honor?

His old dom, whom these people called the Bogandur, used to say that honor didn't bring in the bread and butter. Despite that, he was the most honorable of men that Seg knew, his concept of honor not being of the rigid kind. Rather, it adhered to seeking the best solution to any problem that arose.

Without turning, Seg rapped out: "Milsi! Run to the edge of the jungle! Hide! Do not go too far in—"

As he spoke he lifted the bow, drew, released and had another shaft across the stave, nocked, and the bow lifting for the second shot, all in a twinkling.

Milsi said: "If you think I'm going to run off and leave you—"

"I do not want you to be killed." He loosed again, and again with that incredible speed slapped up another shaft and loosed. "Run, Milsi—*please*!"

"No."

"Then I must take you."

"You would not dare!"

His three arrows had knocked over three of the flyers. They were not all apims like him, some were diffs, for he saw Rapas, Brokelsh, a Gon, a couple of malkos.

The saddle birds they flew were brunnelleys, large and powerful, wide-winged, gaudy of coloration in blues and mauves and browns, yellow beaks and clawed scarlet feet. Plates of wafer-thin beaten gold adorned the birds. They swept in over the clearing, and their bandit riders did not bother to shoot down but landed their birds in great wing-ruffling swirls. The men leaped off, screeching, swirling their swords about their heads.

Seg sniffed and shot a fellow through the breastplate, instantly nocked and drew again and shafted his comrade.

Milsi said, "I am not frightened while I am with you, Seg. If—"

"Yes, yes. I can stand here and shoot the rasts. I suppose—"

"That is best."

"Until they come to handstrokes!"

The fighting broke into clumps as the bandits

rushed in. Each member of the expedition fought as custom dictated. Strom Ornol, being at least in this wiser than one might have expected, disdained his rapier and used a hefty cut and thrust sword, swishing the thraxter about with powerful contemptuous blows. Kalu and his Pachaks simply tore into the bandits, ripping them apart whenever they made contact.

Master Exandu, as Seg had rightly observed, hauled out his single-edged sword and hit anybody who came near him. All the time he complained in his loud hectoring whine, but he kept Shanli safely tucked in behind him. Hop became most intemperate, and raged into a whirlwind, knocking bandits over and trompling them in his eagerness to get to the next.

But these were professional bandits—drikingers—and they were used to overcoming opposition. They lived by terrorizing the neighborhood, and stealing what they wanted. The expedition had in their turn taken the treasures away from the mountain hideout. Located by that gruesome apparition of a beautiful evil woman on her throne, the expedition was now about to pay a price for their audacity.

Master Exandu sliced a fellow's arm nearly off, and stumbled back, shrieking: "San Fregeff! For the sweet sake of Beng Sbodine the Mender of Men! Cast a spell! Reduce these cramphs to jelly!"

Fregeff replied in a somber voice, clearly heard through the tumult as a bell tolls through the lowing of cattle.

"The Witch of Loh has negated all spells here save my own self-preservation."

Exandu let out a yell of utter despair, and sloshed a Rapa over the head so that the Rapa's vulturine beak hung all askew and a gouting puff of brown and gray feathers spurted into the air.

The aerial onslaught of the drikingers pressed on. Seg found more and more difficulty in selecting a target who was not involved in handstrokes.

"I can't just stand here, Milsi. You constrain me."

"Look, Seg—" her voice remained firm, the quaver bravely concealed—"here come three of them to kill us."

"Three," grumped Seg, and shot, flick, flick, flick. "Now, Milsi, please. Either go into the jungle or—"

"I think," and there was a comfortableness in her tone. "I think the jungle is much more dangerous. You will not be there."

"Women," said Seg, and sought a target.

He reached up to his quiver, and groped, and brought out a rose-fletched arrow. After nocking it, he reached up and felt, carefully. There was but the one shaft left, and he knew that was a blue-fletched one of the supply with which he'd begun.

He saw Exandu, swishing and swashing, and complaining away. With a quick snap-shot, Seg disposed of the bandit about to jump on Shanli, dropping him a mere foot short of his target. The blood in Seg demanded a more direct participation. . . . He did not nock the blue-fletched arrow. He slid the bow up his left shoulder. He half-turned.

"Milsi! I must go to Exandu's aid. The time for shooting is past. Now, you must—"

"I must go with you, Seg!"

There was no time for anything further. The sounds of combat boiled menacingly in the jungle clearing. The raw harsh stink of spilled blood broke through the jungle scents and the aromas of cooking. Shrieks and yells, the tinker-hammer of steel upon steel, the puddling of blood in the trampled mud beneath. . . . Seg ripped out his sword and flung himself forward. Milsi followed hard in his footsteps.

He was barely in time.

Exandu, for all his moaning and groaning, could handle his heavy single-edged blade. But he was not in the same class as the guards, or the bandits.

Seg reached him in time to chop a man down, jump over him and skewer another as he was in the act of bringing an axe down on Exandu's undefended head.

For a brief instant, the fight ebbed away as the two dropped. Seg looked about, glaring, worked up. Exandu emitted a groaning laugh, a weak splutter.

"I think they run."

And it was so.

Milsi did not seem to see the corpses strewn everywhere about the clearing. She possessed a serenity in moments of crisis that warmed Seg. He knew practically nothing of her, of her life, her history, and it was most positively certain that she knew nothing of his. Yet, as Kregans say, they had been shafted by the same bolt of lightning at the moment of their meeting. If fate was to be held responsible, then fate would rejoice in their meeting. In the great circle of vaol-paol, the infinite circle of existence, they had met and the circle was complete.

The remaining bandits scrambled into their saddles. The brunnelleys fluttered and scooped

wingfuls of air, soared flapping aloft. The birds
whose riders had been slain joined in the departure.

"By Vox!" said Seg. He leaped for the nearest
bird.

His clutching fingers almost reached the dangling clerketer, the harness which held the rider
securely upon the saddle. The bird twitched a
beady eye on him, reared away, flapped his wings
madly. With a gouting of broken stems and leaves
and detritus, the bird was airborne. He lifted away
and as he went he let rip a squawk that, to Seg at
least, came as a mocking screech of triumph.

"Bad cess to it!" shouted Seg. He stood, hands
on hips, head upflung, staring as the birds bore
away through the radiance of the twin suns.

Walking across to him, Milsi also looked up.

"You know about these wonderful birds, Seg?"

"Something."

"They are very strange to us here in Pandahem.
Yet I have heard of them, of birds and animals that
carry people through the sky. And now I have seen
them. I wonder where they could have come from?"

"From Cottmer's Caverns, that's where, the
damned un-natural things." Hop the Intemperate
looked up, and in his face the look was one of
bafflement. "What could you have done with one,
Pantor Seg, had you caught it?"

"Why," said Seg, surprised. "Flown the thing,
of course. What else?"

"You can fly a bird?"

Seg sobered. He made himself hum and haw.

"We-ell—I could have tried!"

"You'd have fallen off. A copper ob to a golden
crox, you'd have toppled head over heels."

"Aye," agreed Seg, routine caution at last returning to him. "Aye, Hop. Probably."

The fact that the jungle clearing lay encumbered with corpses had different effects upon each of the people there. Most were inured by terrors to a dour acceptance of what might befall. They gave thanks to their various gods that they were not numbered among the slain.

As for clearing up—"

"Leave them all," ordered Strom Ornol, striding about, still wrought up, brilliant and commanding. "Pack everything we need at once. We are leaving now."

"Strom Ornol!" Exandu waddled up. Shanli was busily cleaning his single-edged sword. "We cannot leave our poor fellows unburied, unhallowed."

"We can. The jungle will bury them for us. You know that."

"I know that. But it is not right—"

"Then you may remain here and perform your religious observances, while we march through the Snarly Hills and out of here."

"As to that—"

Seg took no part in this altercation. Like any professional warrior, any Bowman of Loh, he went about the clearing seeking his targets. He drew his knife. Cutting the arrows out had to be done carefully. He might hack a chunk of flesh away, all bloody and dripping; he had to harden himself against that. The most important item was not to damage the arrow.

Milsi did not join him during this proceeding.

During this recovery process, Seg took automatic reckoning of his shots, their effect, the accuracy of his aim.

He realized as he worked that he missed the wagers he and his old dom would have as they shot in the midst of combat. That was not a cruel or insensitive habit. They understood perhaps a little more of what possessed a man in a battle than most. There was absolutely no doubt in Seg's mind, no doubt whatsoever, that he sorely missed his blade comrade, the man these people called the Bogandur.

Kalu and his Pachaks did what any sensible mercenary would do, and helped themselves to the best of their fallen enemy's weaponry.

"Although, Seg, these drikingers use parlous poor weapons. All Krasny work. Look at this spear! The point wouldn't puncture a maiden—"

"Aye, Kalu. And their bows, which to our untold advantage they did not use, are crossbows."

Kalu laughed his Pachak laugh.

"You are not a crossbowman, Seg."

"Oh," sniffed Seg. "I have been known to use a crossbow."

The expedition had lost a number of guards in this fight. The slaves had run screaming, and now some of them returned. Some appeared to have run too far into the jungle, for they did not return. Ornol expressed his great distaste. "If they are a monster's breakfast, that is what serves them right. But it leaves us short of porters."

Seg could not stop himself.

"We're only carrying treasure, after all."

Ornol's pallid face turned on him like the head of a dinosaur above the swampy vegetation, seeking prey.

"You are above taking treasure, are you? You can joke about so important a matter? Perhaps you can afford to be disdainful of gold and gems, Seg the Horkandur!''

Milsi put a hand neatly on Seg's arm.

''Oh, no, pantor. It is not that. Seg but thinks of the provisions we must carry to take us safely through the perils of the Snarly Hills.''

''As for me,'' quoth Exandu, scarlet, puffing, ''I can barely drag my poor old bones along. Oh, how my joints ache! They are on fire—Shanli—''

''I am here, master, with a potion of Mistress Cliomin's Marrow Virtue—you will be eased in no time.''

''Oh, Shanli—you are my treasure!''

''And that,'' said Seg, sotto voce to Milsi, ''is Erthyr's sweet truth!''

The slaves set to to pack up the camp.

''Erthyr?'' said Milsi. ''That is—''

''He is the Supreme Being,'' Seg told her. ''Well, of Erthyrdrin, that is. You believe in Pandrite, of course, being of Pandahem?''

''Of course. I do not call myself an overly religious woman. But I know of the power religion can afford. Pandrite is the most powerful god in Pandahem, as Armipand is the most powerful devil. But there are many other gods and many other pantheons. I have heard you speak of Vox, and of Opaz—''

''Aye.''

She half-lifted one eyebrow at him; he did not elaborate.

They walked a little apart from the others, for Seg carried everything he possessed with him. Like him, Milsi had no retainers. What they could not carry they could not have.

In the end the adventurers sorted out their bundles.

Slaves carried more than slaves cared to carry. The guards, with a deal of haggling over increased rates of pay, agreed to carry bundles. The threat of the pack of toilcas remained with everyone. If that eerie witch woman in her throne could detect them and direct the bandits to them, surely she might do the same for the toilcas?

"She looked at each one of us," said Fregeff. Rik Razortooth upon his shoulder stirred a membraneous wing and crept forth from the sorcerer's voluminous hood. "She searched for someone, that is clear."

"Well, we're all here," pointed out Kalu. He and his men were loaded with loot. That was their profession, venturing into tombs for treasure. They were good at their chosen task in life.

"Perhaps she looked for someone she knew, a friend, or something," said Exandu, a trifle querulously. "And when she saw us she didn't like us hanging about here."

"And we are not hanging about for long!" Ornol had unearthed a whip from his baggage, and now he cracked this with a fearsome bang.

"March! We put a long distance between us and this devilish Coup Blag before nightfall. March!"

Idly, Seg wondered what might happen if the strom accidentally flicked one of the principals with that whip. Or, come to that, if in his arrogant way he mistook a guard under a bundle for a porter and tickled him up . . .

That should prove amusing, at the least, by Orestorio with the Broken String!

During the fight the Lady Ilsa, Strom Ornol's traveling companion, had hidden beneath a heaped-up pile of baggage. Her corn-colored hair had never recovered from her experiences, along with the others of the expedition, in the Coup Blag, and was now a fluffy yellow mass badly in need of the attentions of a first-class hairdresser. The neatness of Milsi's hair, the severe smartness of Shanli's, were in marked contrast.

Shanli carried her accustomed burdens. Milsi had taken a part of Exandu's baggage, after a sidelong look at Seg, who humped along with a massive chest on his shoulder, out of the way of his bowstave. That chest was Exandu's. They owed the merchant nothing, of course; they carried these things out of comradeship.

The Lady Ilsa walked along freely, the new clothes she had discovered in the bandits' hideout flowing about her, her head up, unencumbered.

Well, Seg reflected not a little sourly, the silly girl fancied she was a great lady, and the very first time he'd met her she'd treated him like a slave, like dirt.

The memory cheered him up and he smiled. Milsi observed this. She did not sigh. She did realize that this craggy man with the smooth suppleness of a superb athlete had a past, just as she had. She felt for him sensations new and strange to her. She might not be frightened—too much—by a ferocious onslaught of drikingers out to slay the men and capture the women; she was deeply disturbed by her own fascination with Seg and by the turmoil of her feelings. She consciously used the word turmoil, for that word was often quoted by the poets, and used in the many plays she loved, to denote a woman's perplexities.

A turmoil of emotions had never meant much to her before, rather, she had experienced anger and resentment, for her life had not been easy. Now she was beginning to grasp a little at what the poets meant.

For a woman in her position to fall in love— actually to commit that gross folly!—would be disastrous.

And to fall in love with a wild, reckless, head-strong warrior of fortune would be the stupidest act of all.

So the expedition set off and left the horrors of the Coup Blag and struck boldy down into the Snarly Hills.

# CHAPTER THREE

## Milsi expresses
## a considered opinion

The bold expedition had set off, full of high hopes, from the tavern called The Dragon's Roost in Selsmot. That was a small place, a stockaded area of thatched huts and houses, open and free to the air, rather grand, all things considered, to aspire to the title of town. The smot in the name might cause offense or ridicule in other folk more used to the smots of civilized places out of the jungle.

"I do not particularly wish to go to Selsmot," said Milsi quietly to Seg as they traipsed along a vague trail through the jungle.

"Oh? Well, everyone else started from The Dragon's Roost, and naturally they wish to return there. From Selsmot I suppose they'll all go off home."

"Or to more adventuring. The Pachaks, for whom I have a high regard, are indeed a most interesting party. Fancy! They make their living going around and robbing tombs—"

Seg cleared his throat.

"I'm not sure they'd appreciate your dubbing their profession a robbery. They don't just dig up graves and take away the gravegoods. Far from it. They venture into dungeons and caverns and perils where the owners set traps, both physical and sorcerous, to slay them. I'd say they earn their living. And, anyway, the whole business is a kind of game."

The trail wended past immense trees, each one isolated by its own capacity to discourage rival growths, and the way was relatively easy. Milsi looked up at Seg, and shook her head, and tut-tutted.

"When someone is out to kill me, I hardly call that a game!"

"It's not an unreasonable way of looking at it, though. At least, it helps to take the edge off the horror."

"All the same. They are stealing treasure which is not theirs."

"As I just said, my lady, if they merely robbed graves then I would agree with you. But the owners of the dungeons and tombs the Pachaks visit agree to a kind of compact with the intruders. It goes something like this: 'If you venture in here after treasure, then I will try to trap you. If you win through, you are welcome to what you have found.' In my reckoning, a great many parties of adventurers never do get out alive."

She lifted her shoulder at this.

"I suppose you are right."

"I have heard of a place called Moderdrin, where the land is studded with mounds covering immense dungeons. There the wagers go on all the time. It is well known that parties fly in from all over Paz."

"Paz?"

Seg looked at her in astonishment.

"What, my lady?"

"Paz. What is Paz."

Seg almost groaned aloud. If his old dom were to be here and listen to this!

He explained.

"The grouping of continents and islands on this side of Kregen is called Paz. It includes this island of Pandahem, and the island of Vallia—"

She fired up at once.

"Don't talk to me of Vallia! A vile lot! They're worse pirates than those drikingers from whom we've just won free. Vallia, indeed!"

"Well, my lady, that is as may be. Paz contains the three continents of Havilfar, Segesthes and Turismond, and also the continent of Loh, which is barely regarded these days after the collapse of the ancient Empire of Loh."

"You surprise me, Seg. How do you come to know all this, or are you merely amusing yourself at my expense?"

He didn't even bother to deny the charge.

"I know, my lady, because the union of all the countries and peoples of Paz is essential if we are to face the dangers of those who raid us all."

"You speak of the Schturgins?"

"If you mean the fish-headed reivers who sail up from the other side of the world and slay and burn all our peoples and places, yes. They are variously called Shants, Schtarkins, Shanks. Usually, they are killed whenever the opportunity offers. But they are very hard to slay."

"I have heard of them only. As I said, I do not wish to go to Selsmot or this Dragon's Roost which sounds a most deplorable tavern. I am from farther inland, upriver, where the jungle no longer chokes everything, and the plains are free. . . ."

She stopped abruptly.

Seg could guess she was homesick for the superior climate farther north, nearer to the massive mountain chain that bisected Pandahem in an east-west direction.

He said, bending to her as they walked along: "I have nothing to detain me in Selsmot. Do you know the way to wherever it is you wish to go?"

"No questions, Seg?"

"Are questions necessary?"

"No. I find myself hardly believing in you."

He wrinkled up his eyebrows at this. He was not fool enough, after what had passed between them in the unspoken way of growing confidence, to think she meant she did not believe what he said. But he shied away from the idea of thinking that her disbelief stemmed from what she obviously meant, that he was her perfect jikai.

Seg had seen the folly of boasting. He had seen the idiocy of bloated self-esteem. This idiot Strom Ornol, for all his high-handed ways, was a mere beginner in the league of self-lovers and worshippers of their own importance.

Like a painted and caricatured devil, popping up through a trapdoor in one of the knockabout farces they loved in Vondium, the capital of Vallia, Strom Ornol came storming back down the line of marching men and women. He let his whip lick about, stinging a buttock here, striping a back there. He saw Seg.

By this time they were all aware of Ornol's penchant for quarreling. He thrived on it. No one reacted to his goading these latter days of the expedition, and this infuriated him the more. But the Lady Milsi was a newcomer, brought out of capture within the mountain.

"The drikingers did not fight particularly well, did they, Pantor Seg?"

Seg became cautious on the instant. "Perhaps they were out of practice, Strom Ornol. Mayhap they had not met real fighting men for some time."

Ornol had him in his verbal trap now. Seg's caution came from the way Ornol addressed him as pantor. Both he and the Bogandur had been recognized as lords out for adventure; their particular titles and claims to lands were left vague. Now Seg realized he had opened the way for Ornol to release the venom troubling him.

"Real fighting men? Oh, yes, of course. I, personally, slew four of them. I saw the Pachaks fighting well, as Pachaks always do. Even Master Exandu managed to knock two of the bandits over. But I was not aware of your presence, Pantor Seg, until the very end. I believe you managed two, did you not, when it was all over?"

Seg did not laugh in the popinjay's face.

He was thinking that a quiet, easy reply would be best. In the old days, he'd have just given the idiot a slap around the face and dared him to carry the matter further. These days, his recklessness had been much tempered by hard-won experience.

So that he was completely unprepared for Milsi's outburst.

"Four, you slew, did you, Ornol? Four of them! A great total! Why, Pantor Seg the Horkandur here slew four of them before anybody turned around. And then he shafted four more. Aye! And slew the last two you spoke of and the only two you happened to see.''

Ornol's pallid face froze.

Seg did not bother to sigh. He didn't think with any regrets of the loss of companionship on the march back to civilization. He just dumped down Exandu's burden, took Milsi's bundle from her and threw that down.

As he was doing this, Milsi went on in a voice that cut like best Valkan steel.

''Why, you great bloated buffoon! Don't you understand anything? You're just a barrel of lard rendered down fine and dribbling over the pantry floor! Onker! Idiot! You owe your lives to Pantor Seg!''

Seg grabbed her around the waist, using his left hand. Ornol was ripping out his rapier in such an access of anger he fouled the draw, and struggled and cursed with his baldric. What he would have done had he drawn the rapier Seg did not dare to contemplate by reason of his own reply.

He just stuck his knobby fist into Ornol's jaw.

The dandy lord fell down, his mouth half-open and gargling. Seg didn't bother to hit him again. Guards were running up, yelling. No doubt he'd manage to kill a lot of them before they did for him; that was merely a foolish path. With Milsi to protect, he had to be clever and cunning, rather than brainless and muscle-bound.

Without a word he bundled Milsi up, carrying her bodily with his left arm around her waist.

He wanted to take a wager with himself that he'd reach the jungle edge before they shafted him.

He ran. He nipped between the tree trunks,

using their gigantic boles to give him cover against
the cruel iron birds. Suns light glowed above and
the undergrowth of the rain forest opened up.
Thankfully, Seg plunged into the choking green
thickness, forcing his way past bushes and scrub,
fending off thorned vines, smelling new stinks,
feeling his feet squelching into mud, battling on.

Milsi hit him over the head.

"Put me down, you great lummox! We can get
on more swiftly if I run too."

He plunked her down onto her feet so that her
moccasins slurped deep into the mud.

"All right. Keep moving on, and don't talk."

"Yes, certainly—"

"Shastum!"

At that harsh command to keep silence she bit
her lip. Then she started off to follow him.

Seg was not at all surprised to feel her hand grip
round inside his belt as she hung on as he forged
ahead.

The nature of the forest changed. Gone were the
tall solemn trees with each giant isolated and deny-
ing life to lesser growths. Now the deciduous trees
clustered, tangled and thickly growing, admitting
light here and there and each fighting a long-drawn
struggle for existence. Epiphytes twined about
everywhere, sucking sustenance from the trees,
and vines depended, looping, sensile, as ravenous
to eat as any predator.

Over the centuries the trees shed their leaves
into a deep congestion upon the floor of the forest.
The leaves took time to rot down. The smell rose
high, thick, cloying, a stench that gagged. Seg and
Milsi moved on more through than over a giant
compost heap.

The way grew hard and more hard.

Presently Seg halted.

He found a niche where a many-rooted tree left a space beneath the out-branching roots. Dampness cloyed. They were both sweating. Their clothes clung unpleasantly to them. Seg was not at all sure that the space beneath the roots was safe. A vine looped down inquisitively and he lopped the end with a slash from his sword. Milsi jerked back.

"Keep still, do not speak, and keep your eyes open."

Dumbly, she nodded.

She had known this warrior to be sudden and quick; now she was seeing a new side to his character.

Seg peered about. He felt confident that any pursuit would have given up by now, especially when the pursuers hit the choking, dense, almost impenetrable forested area. The heat was stifling. Insects buzzed and pirouetted everywhere. Pinheads clustered and started to suck blood. Seg and Milsi, cautiously, kept on slapping them away.

As for Milsi, she could barely comprehend how she had contrived to find herself in such a terrible predicament.

What would her people say if they could see her now!

She had to persevere. She could tell this warrior Seg the Horkandur much; she knew she could not bring herself to tell him all. Not yet, at least. . . .

A monster, all teeth and scales and spikes, blundered past, forcing his way through the tangle by bulk and power. Even he had to pick a path that avoided the worst of the natural obstructions. Seg and Milsi were quite content to let him pass without comment.

"We will wait here until I am sure no one is following us. Then we will think about a drink and some food."

"Very well, Seg."

So meek, her answer! She surprised herself!

The sounds of the forest rose and fell with the ceaseless activities of life and death. The heat sweltered. The great red sun, Zim, and the smaller green sun, Genodras, cast down a muted, entangled radiance among the fronds and branches. The pinheads stung and were slapped away with increasing irritation.

Presently, Milsi said, "You mentioned something about eating and drinking, Seg."

"Aye."

"Well?"

Her question was not so much tart as resignedly amused, as though she was waiting expectantly for a miracle.

Patiently, keeping a continuing observation along the backtrail and all about the tangled root mass, Seg told her: "Food is no problem. As for drink, we must boil every drop of water we touch."

"I see."

She waited, sharing his patience.

Then: "Do we eat and drink now?"

"Wait."

"But—"

Still he did not look at her. He sat comfortably, relaxed and yet, as she could clearly see, immensely alert. He was so still as to appear graven from stone, the only movement the occasional impatient flick of a finger to ward off the pestering pinheads.

"Listen, Lady Milsi. In the jungle—or anywhere else, come to that—patience equals life. Impatience equals death."

"I do understand—"

"I think not."

She bit her lip in vexation. What a crude barbarian warrior he was! And yet, well, this was a part of his life she had not shared, could not have shared. The idea that this way of living might be hers from now on gave her a shudder that was not entirely delicious with romantic terror; but was not too far removed from that silly notion.

If she told him the truth about herself, he might react in a wild and unpredictable way that would spoil everything. No. Far better to get back home to safety and then sort things out.

She had no doubts whatsoever that with Seg the Horkandur to protect her she would see her home. She would arrive in the end safely; the trouble was the journey at this rate was going to take an unconscionable amount of time.

At last—at long last—Seg said, "They did not follow us this far. Now we find our meal."

A single shaft brought down a small creature of large ears and thin tail and orange and green furriness. Thankfully, as far as Milsi was concerned, it was a mammal and not a reptile. Brusquely, as Seg set about preparing the poor creature, he instructed Milsi to collect wood and break open the crumbly interior from the outer bark.

He produced his tinderbox from the soft leather pouch attached to his belt and the janul worked splendidly. In a secure cover of a mass of roots affording spying eyes no flicker of flame, Seg got the fire going. The small prepared animal, a forest colo, went on a spit over the fire.

Milsi watched fascinated as Seg's powerful hands molded and worked a chunk of the mud. He fashioned a pot and made it watertight. Water was at the moment no problem for the rains left puddles here and there—which Seg ignored. He climbed a tree alert for any unpleasant denizens with prior rights of habitation, and fetched down a cup-shaped leaf filled with liquid.

This he emptied into his pot and boiled up. It was a messy process, and twice the pot split so that he had to start afresh. But, eventually, Milsi drank water of a brackish and vegetation-tasting quality. It tasted fine.

The little colo went down well.

"Now we march."

"The way is dreadfully hard."

"We follow where these blundering great monsters open a way for us. We go quietly. We listen, and we smell. We will see them before they see us."

"I hope to Pandrite you are not mistaken."

"You can only die once."

"Oh, I agree. But that is one time too many for me."

He smiled, did not answer, and set off.

Although, of course, with the fiendish cunning of some wizards to command unholy skills it might be perfectly possible to die and be resurrected and so die all over again. . . . This prospect was one which displeased Seg enormously. His upbringing, wild and free though it had been, had inculcated in him a respect for the processes of nature.

His respect was genuine and extended universally—save in one thing.

Seg had no respect for anything that interfered with his procurement of the finest bowstaves he could cut.

A vine studded with short hard spikes lashed in from nowhere. A shiny brown spine caught in Milsi's tunic just to the side of her navel and whipped back, tearing the blue cloth around to the small of her back. She yelped, and Seg's single slash dropped the vine onto the forest floor, wriggling and squirming.

"Did it—?"

"No, thank the good Pandrite."

The skin had not been punctured, no blood had been drawn. Very seriously, his face expressionless, Seg shifted the ripped blue cloth aside and inspected Milsi's stomach, side and back. He could see no lacerations in that tanned pink skin. He breathed out a relieved sigh.

"That is one problem of walking down a trail made by the monsters."

"It is still far preferable to struggling through that awful jungle."

As they went on it occurred to Seg to wonder how Milsi's skin under her tunic was so smoothly tanned. Since he had known her she had always had clothes, of some sort or another, rags mostly until the last chamber of the Coup Blag, to cover her. The suns would give you a wonderful tan if you stayed out for a responsible length of time.

Well, when the time was opportune he'd mention it to her. Her answer would probably involve carefree days of sunbathing at home. Her home, he gathered, was situated not in the capital of this land of Croxdrin but, as she had indicated, farther north out in the open plains in Mewsansmot.

There was no chance of conversation as they walked along the monster-opened trail so that much as he would have liked to find out more about her and her history, as any wandering fellow lusted after details of people and places and things, Seg was constrained to follow his own dictum of patience.

He had the map of the area fairly well embedded in his skull. The river, known as the River of Bloody Jaws, looped in an enormous arc around the Snarly Hills. Traffic went by river. The teeth and jaws ferociously at work in the Kazzchun River were not as fearful as the terrors of the forest.

From where they now were any direction other than a heading with west in it would bring them to the river.

North with a touch of easting, he decided, would be best. If the distance to the river was the same no matter in which direction they went, then by going north the distance to cover on the river would be shortened. When they stopped for one of the periodic rests he insisted on, mindful of the husbanding of marching men's—and women's! —strengths, Milsi began prying in order to open up a little more of the story of this fearsome warrior bowman.

"For a start, Seg, how did you come by your cognomen?"

At that Seg laughed out loud.

"Horkandur?" He was clearly delighted by his own thoughts. Milsi smiled in response. She enjoyed being with Seg, and for this space of time at least forgot her own problems in their shared perils.

"I know it means you have gained renown as a great archer—"

"In that, the sobriquet does not lie overmuch, although I detest braggarts. No, my old dom, he whom you know as the Bogandur, gave it to me, when I gave him his nickname. This was when we met up with the expedition at The Dragon's Roost—"

She showed her astonishment.

"But that defies honor! You give each other resounding titles, just like that? Really, Seg, you amaze me."

"We did not wish to give our true names."

"On the run?"

Again he laughed.

"In a fashion; but not from any just pursuit. We felt it more prudent. My name is Seg Segutorio."

Very gravely she inclined her head, and said: "Lahal, Seg Segutorio."

"Lahal, my Lady Milsi. And the rest of your name?"

Her smile faltered.

A flutter seized her, so that she looked up, and exclaimed at the sight of two bright red eyes staring down at them from a branch of a nearby tree. Seg looked and saw the little furry body, the tail wrapped about a thinner twig, and said: "Another little colo. Perhaps we will have to eat his cousin tonight. For now, he is safe."

The pathetic interlude gave her time to decide what to say.

"My father's name was Javed Erithor the Good.

My mother's name was Natema Parlaix. I may use either name, as I wish."

"I know of the custom. In Erthyrdrin we have a different system of naming of names. I was able to assume the honor of the torio when my father died. He, too, was a good man, if a trifle reckless—"

"Like his son?"

"Oh, aye. But I learn. When I die my son, my eldest son, Drayseg, will become Seg Segutorio."

She felt a distinct stab at her heart.

"You have children? You are married?"

Seg's face abruptly took on the look of a sky at nightfall, before a thunderstorm. She did not flinch back; had she done so no one watching would have been surprised.

"I am blessed with a family of three, and, yes, I was married."

"Oh—I am sorry."

"I will tell you. But we have rested enough. We must push on."

"Of course."

Only when they were once more marching along the blundering monster's trail did she think to wonder just where his family might be now, what place in all of Kregen they called home. Seg— who was Seg Segutorio—had taken on a new dimension. He remained a wild and reckless wandering warrior; but he had roots.

As for Seg he was trying to puzzle out the inner meaning of the names of Milsi's family. They did not sound Pandahemic names.

# CHAPTER FOUR

## Diomb and Bamba

A clattering commotion broke out ahead along the trail. A trilling noise as of a cage full of parakeets all shrilling away and fluttering their wings against the bars of the cage mingled with sharper shrieks of rage and pain.

Seg put out a hand to halt Milsi and she walked on for a moment so that her stomach pressed against Seg's sinewy palm. She was highly conscious of the contact; Seg did not notice.

He stared evilly along the trail, tensed ready for action and yet perfectly relaxed. When he had sized up the situation out there his brain would tell his muscles what to do. They would respond instantly. That was the secret, albeit a simple one, of readiness for action.

Presently, as the uproar continued unabated, without gaining or losing volume, he padded cautiously forward. He kept to the side of the trail, and he whispered so that no one more than two or three paces away could overhear.

"Watch for those dratted killer vines, Milsi."

"Oh—yes!"

The trail bent here as the monster who had made it failed to break through a tree all of five hundred seasons old. With his side against the tree, Seg peered cautiously around, and along the farther extent of the trail.

What he saw filled him with astonishment. Milsi joined him, and sucked in her breath, and said: "They are dinkus. Savage. They used poisoned darts."

"So I see."

The dinkus appeared to be caught up in a situation at once horrific and comic. They were pygmies. Each dinko stood about one meter tall, built like an apim, with the exception that from the cunningly fashioned shoulder blades swung four arms instead of two. Each man was stark naked apart from a bark apron.

They did use poisoned darts, which they shot from blow pipes.

They were engaged in a fight between two different tribes, as was evident from the colors of the feathers they wore in their clay-matted hair, and their private fight had been interrupted by a toilca. Therein lay the comic aspect of the horror. To a dinko a toilca was a monstrous beast.

"I really do think this is no concern of ours, Milsi."

"You are right. Yet they are so—and they cannot shoot their darts at the toilca's scales and hope to penetrate."

Looking out, Seg saw that the toilca had already ripped up or squashed half a dozen of the dinkus.

The two opposing parties had, perforce, joined forces to fight the monster. Seg made up his mind.

He stepped out into the center of the trail.

"Hai!"

So wrapped up in the combat were most of the pygmies that they did not hear him. Some did. They swiveled to stare down the trail, and the long blow-pipes switched up most evilly.

"Hai!"

And Seg loosed twice, swift accurate shots that punched clean through the eyes of the toilca under the horny protecting scales. The monster lashed about, writhing, and the pygmies leaped for their lives.

With bow ready, arrow nocked and the shaft half drawn, held by his left hand, Seg walked forward. He lifted his right hand.

"Llahal! I trust I have helped you, friends."

They chattered out, parakeets flinging their wings at a cage. Their voices chittered.

Then one with the most feathers in his matted hair stepped forward. Instantly another stepped up alongside the first. He wore just about as many feathers, but they were red as the first's were blue.

"Hai! Llahal. Are you friend?"

The blue-feathered pygmy was not to be left in the shade.

"Hai! Answer me quickly, or you die!"

"Now hold on," shouted Seg. "Just hold on a minute. I've shot the poor dratted toilca for you. I do not expect much in the way of thanks, but I do expect a little friendship—"

"No boltim is a friend to any dinko."

"Boltim?"

"That means big man," whispered Milsi.

"I know that—oh, I see. Yes." Seg retained that cunning archer's left-handed grip on bow and shaft.

"I may be a boltim. I bear you no ill will. By the Veiled Froyvil! I could have passed by and you'd all be dead, chomped up by that monster!"

The fellow with the red feathers said: "That is true, by Clomb of the Ompion Never-Miss."

"Whoever he and it may be," said Seg—to himself.

Blue feathers wasn't so sure.

"You speak with a false tongue," he started.

"And if I had not spoke you'd be quietly digesting in that toilca's insides. Why, man, he could eat all of you and look around for more!"

"Seg!"

Assuredly, that had not been a politic thing to say.

Seg blustered on.

"We are just taking a little stroll along here, doing no harm to anyone, least of all you, noble dinkus. We have helped you. Now we will go on our way and give you the remberees."

A chattering gobble of argument among the pygmies followed. They spoke the universal Kregish that had been imposed on the world, heavily adulterated by accent and local dialect words. They began to form up into two separate bands. Beside the long blowpipes and the quivers of darts slung over their shoulders by straps they carried cudgels. These were, by ordinary standards, puny. If one laid alongside the head of one dinko powered by the angry muscles of another, the results could be fatal.

Seg did not speak again.

He slowly withdrew to the tree, and stood, silently, watching. Before very long tribal hatreds flared up. The red feathers and the blue feathers started off, bashing at one another. And Seg noticed a curious fact. They did not puff out their cheeks into twin balloons and blow darts tipped with poison at one another. They slung the blowpipes down or over their backs and started in a-slugging one another with the cudgels. He understood what he was seeing. This was survival of the species, survival of the dinkus, against the perils of their home in the jungle.

Presently the fight was of such an intensity that he and Milsi could edge along on the fringe of the trail and pass by without any one of the battling pygmies bothering his head about them.

They reached the far side of the conflict and turned to rejoin the trail out of sight of the dinkus.

Seg fell over a couple of naked bodies entwined beside a bush. He staggered and regained his balance with the litheness of a cat. The blowpipe quivered three inches from his chest, the lad's cheeks distended like twin red apples.

Without hesitation Seg's left hand holding bow and arrow swished around, deflected the blowpipe. The lad expelled his breath in a mighty gasp and the dart shot off into the jungle. At once a shrill squawk sounded.

Seg said, "I hear you hit your target then, my lad. For, of course, you were not shooting at me, were you?"

His gaze beat down on the pygmy lad. He was a young dinko, and he was cuddling up to a younger dinka, who still lay by the bush, rigid with terror.

"No," said the lad. He swallowed. He looked

up and up to this monstrous boltim who towered like an ancient tree of the forest. "No."

"That is wise."

"Oh, the poor things!" exclaimed Milsi. She came forward in a rush and gathered the girl up and cradled her as she might a child. The girl was crying.

"So that's the way of it, then," observed Seg.

He sighed. Sex and passion and tribal taboos had played tricks with Kregen's past, and no doubt would continue to do so into the future.

The lad wore red feathers.

The girl wore blue feathers.

"They will surely part us if they find us," said the boy. He spoke up bravely. "If they do not kill us."

"I do not think they would kill you. Life has to be precious to anyone living in the forest and fighting its perils."

"You don't know them—they are rigid as a petrified tree. Blood lines, inheritance, taboos—and I love Bamba."

The girl Bamba, cradled in Milsi's arms, sniffled out: "And I love Diomb."

Seg released the arrow grip and stowed the shaft. He was not about to allow himself to become embroiled in the half-comical, half-tragical affairs of these little people of the forest.

"Well," he said with some brutality. "I don't know what you two were doing. But if you can't go home to your tribes you'll have to run away. I wish you well."

"We were running away and they caught us. Then the toilca came along, and—"

"The toilca is dead and your respective tribes

are trying to bash each other's brains out. You'd better cut along sharpish.''

"Oh," wailed the girl. "Would that Clomba of the Fruit Tree Eternal would aid us now!"

The pygmy lad, naked save for a bark apron, clutching his blowpipe, stared up at Seg. His face was formed pleasingly, with regular features, and his dark eyes showed a bright intelligence. Just as Seg was telling himself that any eyeball can shine up nicely, that does not mean its owner has any brains at all, Diomb rapped out as though a bottle-cork burst from the neck: "We were running away. We were going to cross the river and seek our fortune. We can come with you. That is excellent."

"Do what?"

"Why, boltim, Bamba and me will walk with you. Together we can see the wide world."

"Oh, aye!"

Milsi spoke up and shattered Seg afresh.

"Oh, yes, Seg! Do let them come." Then, forgetting for the moment where she was, she added: "I shall take Diomb and Bamba with me. They are very welcome."

Seg looked at the Lohvian longbow in his left fist. He shook his head. Then he shoved the bow up onto the peak of his shoulder, snapped it fast, turned about and said, "Very well! Let them come. And you take care of them, my Lady Milsi."

She flared up at this, angry, and yet despairing of ever making any man see sense.

"I shall! Do not fret over that, Seg Segutorio!"

# CHAPTER FIVE

## Out of the Snarly Hills

In the time it took them to march through the
forest to the River of Bloody Jaws, Seg was forced
to admit to himself that the dinkus, Diomb and
Bamba, proved themselves to be a fine addition to
the little party. They knew this place, for it was
their home. Diomb had only recently gone through
the mysteries and ordeals of manhood and emerged
as a dinko hunter. Bamba and he were quite clearly
intoxicated with each other.

That was very nice for them—now.

Seg scowled a bit, and looked loweringly on
Milsi, who, for her part, disdained to notice.

When they heard up ahead the clink and clatter
of bottles and glasses, the apparent murmur of
happy human voices, Diomb brightened up.

He was a mischievous fellow. He glanced up
sideways at Seg, half-laughing.

"Ah, Seg, do you hear that? Friends are waiting
for us."

Seg had enough human tolerance to wait awhile

before believing the dinko meant what he said.
The sounds reached them from beyond a screen of
vegetation, for the forest appeared more open here
and they knew by this that they must be nearing
the river. The trackways criss-crossed, and not by
man but by the increasing number of animals living here.

"Friends?" said Seg. He decided to play along
with Diomb for a time. "They sound as though
they are having a good time. And I could do with
a wet."

"A wet?"

Seg smiled in his turn. There were so many
things these pygmies did not know. Their life was
primitive. They had a lot to learn.

"Yes. A drink of something other than water. It
*sounds* as though up there they have plenty of
bottles."

Diomb caught the inflexion in Seg's voice.

"Yes, Seg. Bottles. I know of them but have
never seen one. They must have some over there."

"Well, then, I suggest you toddle along and
ask."

Seg stopped beside the bush and looked down
on Diomb. He quite expected the pygmy to stop,
also. Then there would be a crestfallen explanation.
For, of course, there were no happy drinkers up
ahead celebrating. The clinking sounds, the mur-
murous voices, were produced by a killer plant
known to civilized men as the Cabaret Plant. What
the dinkus called it Seg didn't know, and was not
just at the moment particularly interested to find
out.

Instead, boldly, Diomb marched out past the
bush and into the clearing.

Seg watched.

Out there in its cleared area the Cabaret Plant carried on its audio-pantomime. The sounds were remarkably realistic. To a forest-dwelling dinko who hadn't even seen a bottle or glass, the sounds must come as mysterious and evocative. The plant itself was a fine full grown specimen.

The gourd-shaped main body was capacious enough to hold three or four people. The sounds of voices trilling and laughing and the clink of bottle against glass increased in intensity. From the top of the gourd rose a tall stem crowned with an orange flower. Seg's lips drew tightly together.

He drew his sword.

Diomb carried a large leaf plucked from a greenish-blue low-growing bush and as he stepped out he bent his legs, his knees like springs, and he moved gently from side to side.

The orange flower lashed.

It swept viciously down toward the pygmy. As it struck it opened wide to reveal its flower-petalled head encrusted with spines.

The deadly orange flower slashed at Diomb. He waited, then sprang swiftly to the side, trailing the leaf which was smashed full out of his hand. He darted back, and his face blazed with pride and prowess.

"Hai!" cried Bamba, glowing with reciprocal pride.

"Huh," grunted Seg, sourly. "Some of the tribal fun and games, is it? Proving you're a man among men?"

"More than that, Seg." Diomb waited, judged his moment exactly, and darted in, snatched up the leaf and withdrew. The orange flower lashed about in baffled frenzy.

"I have never done that before," remarked Diomb. "I have practiced, of course, with my friends slashing at me and pretending to be the Naree-Giver."

"It was well-done, Diomb," declared Milsi, with a glance at Seg that put him in his place.

"All right, Diomb," said Seg, almost growling. "I knew what was what the moment we heard the Cabaret Plant. What you call a Naree-Giver." He looked at the leaf which Diomb was now most carefully inspecting. "Narees, is it? This is how you come by the poisoned darts for your blow-pipes?"

"This is one way, yes."

The leaf was struck through by the poisoned spines from the plant. There must have been thirty of them. Now Diomb began a painstaking removal of each spine, putting them into a bark pouch in his apron.

"We splice the spine to the main shaft of the naree. These will make very good weapons, you will see."

"I daresay."

Seg decided not to feel chastened. He'd had a nasty experience with a Cabaret Plant before, and he'd been classing them as among the more hideous of the horrors of the jungle. And here this little pygmy lad trotted along and baited the ferocious plant and took from it its spines to use as his blow-pipe darts—and had the effrontery to give the thing a name that indicated the esteem in which he held it! Enough to make a bluff tough fighting man spit.

The last Cabaret Plant Seg had encountered had cost him ten gold pieces. . . .

Milsi broke into his thoughts with a pert suggestion that it was high time they stopped for something to eat.

Diomb's skills as a forest hunter provided ample food. Water continued to be boiled. They selected a good campsite and settled down. By the signs within the forest they hoped to reach the river on the morrow, or the next day.

Seg inquired if Diomb shot his dinner with his poisoned naree and then ate it, poison and all.

"We usually snare our food, as I have done since we met. But if we have to shoot with a poisoned naree there are ways of boiling or baking the poison out. I can bring a small quarry down with an unpoisoned dart, of course."

"Oh, of course."

Milsi gave him a look.

When they had eaten, Seg felt that a small rest would be in order. He wanted to know more of Milsi's life story, yet he was reluctant to press too hard. He did not wish to reveal very much about his own life, for that would take a clever man to explain and a trusting woman to believe, by Vox!

"Seg," she said as they lay side by side, some way apart from the two dinkus who were out of sight together. "Why are you so hard on Diomb?"

"Hard? Me, hard on the little fellow?"

"Perhaps you are jealous of him?"

The torrent of images, desires, passions that flared into Seg's brain made him almost gasp aloud. He rolled over and stared off into the forest, away from Milsi. He was vividly aware of her presence at his side. Jealous? He was conscious of all that he was missing, that until his meeting with Milsi he had banished from his life. Well, now was the time to tell her a few home truths that might explain a little more. . . .

"I told you I was once married."

"Yes."

"My wife was called Thelda. She was a—a funny woman. She always meant well. I could see how she tried. Yet—"

Milsi could not see his face. She said: "You need not explain, Seg, if it is painful. I think I understand. One meets these people in life who mean so well, and yet whose every effort turns to disaster."

He rolled over to look at her.

"Well—it wasn't disaster all the time! No. I won't have that. I loved Thelda. I truly did. We had a good life together, and there were the children, and our friends, and life to be lived."

"And she died. I am sorry, truly sorry."

"I thought she had died."

"Oh?"

"There was a difficult period. We called it the Time of Troubles. We were separated. I was sore wounded. I searched for Thelda, searched for her where I knew she would be, and then in our home. I could not find her. I was made slave—"

"Oh, Seg!"

"It was not pleasant. My old dom hoicked me out of that and I had to spend time recovering from my wound and, well, everyone said Thelda was dead. So I believed it, too."

"And she wasn't?"

"I got over Thelda. I said I could not continue to love a ghost, a person broken from the ib. I put her out of my mind. But I did not look at another woman. I was a husk, you see, until . . ." He stopped, and plucked a thin twig from the bush by which they lay and stuck it between his teeth. He chewed reflectively.

Milsi said nothing.

"Only recently my old dom told me that Thelda was alive. She believed me to be dead, as I believed her. She had found a man, a man I knew slightly, an honest, upright man. They loved and were married and there was a child. This was done in all honor."

"Oh, Seg!"

"Yes, well, that is all ancient history now."

She felt perplexed.

"You did not say how old your son—Drayseg—was."

While the people of Kregen could live to well beyond two hundred years—if they did not get themselves killed off before then—they did not alter a great deal in appearance from the time they reached maturity to a few years before they died. Despite this there were small signs by which one person could estimate the age of another with fair accuracy. Without this subtle judgment unfortunate liaisons might occur; a passionate romance between a young person of twenty-five with another who looked just the same but was a hundred and twenty-five, might be acceptable to them, might be warmingly wonderful an example of human faith and love, it was also a cruel trick to play on frail humanity by fate.

Milsi wrinkled up her eyebrows at Seg. He was clearly a mature man, strong and craggy, and a man she found undeniably handsome and attractive.

He was a few years older than she was. But he talked as though these events had taken place seasons and seasons ago.

"How old Dray is means nothing," he said at last. "The twins are a bit younger. They're all off in the great wide world adventuring and having fun, I hope, and all my prayers to Erthyr go to protect them from the perils of life."

This was the difficulty, Seg knew, that his old dom had had to face many times. They'd both bathed in the Sacred Pool of Baptism in far Aphrasöe, in the River Zelph, along with their families and good friends. This assured them of a thousand years of life, together with the capacity to recover from wounds with an amazing rapidity. Seg judged Milsi to be a few years younger than he appeared to be, the age he'd been when he and the riotous crew had all flown off to Aphrasöe, the Swinging City. He had grown considerably in judgment and wisdom since then, although, naturally, he was still your wild reckless warrior kind of fellow, to be sure.

He found himself wondering how Thelda would handle the odd circumstances that she did not appear to age as her husband, Lol Polisto, aged. For Thelda, as far as he knew, was not aware that she would live for a thousand years. That was cruel. He would have to rectify that, and, if possible, make arrangements for Lol, also, to take that miraculous baptism. Again and again they'd discussed, in all the various places of Kregen they'd adventured together, he and the Bogandur, just how you dealt with this unexpected gift of a thousand years of life—if gift it was.

There had to be a limit; how to apply that cruel limiting judgment?

Milsi, now . . .

He was about to attempt some blundering pack of lies to explain away this surprising lack of knowledge of his childrens' ages, when Bamba popped out from the bush pushing her bark apron straight, followed at once by Diomb.

"Seg! We must—"

"Now by all the Shattered Targes in Mount Hlabro!" burst out Seg. "What is it now?"

"We must hide. A party of boltim approach, and they may not be friendly."

Seg grunted. "Won't be, more likely."

Keeping low into the bushes, silent, watchful, the little party watched as the newcomers stalked and staggered past.

The Katakis stalked, strutting in heavy boots, flicking their whips and flicking their tails at the coffle of slaves who staggered, struggling on, naked and chained.

Seg counted the Katakis. Twenty of the diffs, twenty fierce, voracious, unpleasant and highly lethal slavers, twenty packets of sudden death. Flared of nostrils, the Katakis, low of frowning forehead, with black hair wild and tangled, with jagged teeth and hungry jaws. They were half-armored and carried spears and swords and bows. They urged on the slaves, who were of many races, without mercy, shouting the ugly word to force on dead-tired muscles and aching limbs.

"Grak, you yetches! Grak!"

Seg thought of Milsi. He thought, also, of Diomb and Bamba. Well, he could shaft half a dozen and then they'd be on him and slay him. That would

not help either the poor devils in the coffle or
Milsi and the dinkus.

So, then. He must perforce crouch here like any
coward and wait until the slavers had passed.

He did not think it necessary to advise Milsi of
his decision. For her part, she stared unseeingly
upon the slaves, shuddered at the predatory Katakis,
kept very silent and fervently prayed that her great
jikai, this warrior Bowman Seg Segutorio, would
not conceive his honor demanded he rush out to
fight and die.

That this illogical behavior might be expected
from Seg was to her the greatest proof of her
irrationality in finding herself in this position. No
sensible person would interfere with slavers about
their business, and most certainly not Katakis. The
bladed steel strapped to their tails whickered like
summer lightning, the flats belaboring the slaves
in vicious spanking buffetings. If those steel blades
turned edge on. . . .

When the miserable coffle had struggled on and
was out of sight and sound, Diomb stretched and
said: "Now, Seg, tell me what that was all about.
I am most anxious to find out about the outside
world. But I own I do not understand what I
saw."

"Those ugly brutes were Katakis, what we call
Whiptails. Steer clear of 'em unless you want
trouble. The slaves were—"

"Slaves?"

Seg tried to explain. Diomb interrupted.

"I know that a person may own certain items—
my blowpipe and darts, my apron. But nothing
much else. The elders have explained much of the
outside world to us, for we are not ignorant savages.

I thought I understood the principle of possession. But owning people—''

''There's a lot in the world you have to learn about,'' said Milsi. ''And I shall be happy to show you and Bamba.''

The trouble with a lot of this wonderful world of Kregen could be summed up in the one word— slavery. Seg had had his run-ins with the diabolical custom and so he could while deploring Milsi's attitude understand it. He did not look forward with any pleasure to what the future held when he began the process of correcting her attitude. He was long past the stage when he consulted his conscience on the matter. He was long past the stage when he worried over the problem of whether or not he had the right to change people's minds on the question of slavery. He had seen enough. He had lost a great deal over the slavery business, quite happily, and he was prepared to go to great lengths to do what he could to stamp out the evil.

He did not doubt that his explanation of slavery would be somewhat different from Milsi's.

A few dwaburs farther on they ran into a marshy area.

''We have the Malar Marshes in Erthyrdrin,'' said Seg. ''I am not enamored of them. We had best find another way around.''

That being agreed, they cut inland a trifle to circumvent the noxious areas.

Milsi chattered away to Diomb and Bamba. Seg strode on silently, biding his time.

When he had an opportunity at the next halt to tell Milsi a thing or three, he found himself instead attempting to explain the nomenclature customs of Erthyrdrin.

"My children may call themselves Segutorio, or Segutoria, as a kind of surname when out of the country. That is, if it fits in with the country's customs. But the Torio is reserved for the eldest, and the first syllables are always the same. The girl child will take her mother's name as a second name, and when she marries may attach her husband's name if she wishes."

He picked a scrap of meat from between his teeth with a sliver of clean stripped wood and not his finger. He was finicky with the operation. Milsi noticed this.

He went on, "My lad Valin, Silda's twin, is called Valin Segutorio at home; but that is not really correct and we would not do so in Erthyrdrin. He—"

"But, Seg. I thought your home was Erthyrdrin? Where is it you call home, then?"

No good for Seg to castigate his loose tongue.

He replied easily enough, and with enough truth to ease his conscience.

"Oh, we have a fine home in Valka. But, as I was saying—"

"Valka? I have not heard of it."

"North of here. But, as I was saying—"

"North?"

Seg sighed. Women were the very devil for sticking to a point you didn't want explored, and likewise the very devil for being loose-minded and scatty when it pleased them. Damned clever, women, usually.

"It's a small island in the Sea of Opaz."

"H'm. It must be a very small island, then, for I know most of the more important ones along the north coast of Pandahem in the Sea of Opaz. Although, Seg, we Pandaheem more often call the sea the Ocean of Panda.''

"Oh, yes, that shows how cut off we are there."

He did not dare to look at her in case she saw the unease in him. The devil Chanko-taroth take it! He did not wish to lie to Milsi; but he didn't want too much of his past to be revealed until he was ready to do the revealing.

Milsi ran swiftly over the major islands whose names she knew up there off the north coast of the main island. Valka? There was a ring in the name, a faint memory of hearing it, spoken in great passion by her father. But the memory would not coalesce.

Around almost all the coasts of Kregen the islands clustered as thickly as bubbles on the surface of boiling milk. There were far too many for all to be recalled at will.

"You were saying?"

"Oh, yes. Valin will never be Valin Valintorio unless he gains great renown, is recognized, can persuade the elders and the secret ones to grant him the torio. Then he will have a family, and lands, and may call himself Valin Valintorio. I look forward to the day."

"And the name Seg will go on through the main line?"

"Just so."

"With us it is different." Then she stopped and bit her lip. "I mean, well, here the male line is recognized only if the female line is in accord."

"That means, exactly?"

"Well, Seg, to give the example that has exercised the minds of everyone in Croxdrin lately. The king, Crox, lost his wife and entire family in a dreadful accident. It was through his wife that his legal entitlement to the crown was established.''

''So he had to look around for the next legal heir?''

''It has been known in the past for fathers to marry their daughters to secure the throne—in name only, I hasten to add. So—''

''Oh, I see. I heard that this poor Queen Mab whom you served was married to the king and he departed in the same hour to this fateful expedition into the Coup Blag. Then Queen Mab followed—she must have loved him, then, although I was told the marriage was political only.''

''It was only political! There was no love there, only a dreadful acceptance of fate.''

''Well, you should know, you were her lady in waiting.''

''Yes.''

''Diomb and Bamba have stopped frisking about and are looking expectant. It is time we moved on.''

Then she surprised him.

''Time is a terrible thing, Seg the Horkandur! I could almost wish this journey, which now is far more pleasant than when we began, could go on forever.''

''But you want to get home to Mewsansmot!''

''I do, I do. And yet . . .''

''Come on, you two!'' called Bamba. ''Diomb is quite impatient in this as in other refined things.''

''Coming.''

Their route to skirt the marshes lay northwest,

north, northeast and then, just to make sure, they curved down a litle and struck along east-northeast.

"And, my fine young friends," quoth Seg, lustily, striding along. "At the first decent hostelry we run across, I shall treat you to roast vosk, momolams, squish pie, and a heaping dish of palines. *And* there will be ale, and wine—believe you me!"

"We had best, perhaps," said Milsi, most anxiously, "be very wary regarding ale and wine for Bamba and Diomb."

"Naturally. But they'll down their jugs with the best in no time, you will see."

"We have strange stories about the dinkus from the forest. We must take care."

"If anyone offers insult to our friends, Milsi—"

"You, Seg Segutorio the Horkandur, had best stay out of stupid arguments until we—"

"Assuredly, my lady," and Seg bowed a deep and most ironical bow.

"Oh, you!" flared Milsi, the color rising.

Seg could well understand what Milsi meant when she said she wished this journey could go on forever. The forest had now become far less hostile, the Snarly Hills dwaburs to the rear. There were few habitations, as most of the villages and towns were located along the river; but there were villages within the forest. The slavers operated here, and that made life terrible. But for the adventurers marching through the forest, eyes and ears alert, the dangers were by now a part of life, accepted by the two apims in the same spirit as the two dinkus.

The air breathed less oppressively. There was

food aplenty, and water—boiled to drink. The life made men and women hardy and inured to hardship. And yet, surely, to a lady brought up as a handmaiden to serve a queen, this rude out-of-doors adventuring life could not hold aught of pleasure? Yet Milsi throve.

Seg, wistful, was reminded of ancient days.

He said, once: "Milsi, do you know the difference between fallimy and vilmy flowers?"

She laughed in an off-hand way. "Of course." Then she saw how serious he was beneath the casual attitude. "One is good for poultices, the other to clean disgusting corroded cesspits and cisterns."

"Yes. And you could tell them apart?"

"Well, would I put a cistern-cleaning poultice on your wound—" She saw him. "Seg!"

"It is all right. I am ashamed. I should not have said anything—"

"Can you tell me?"

"Not now." He walked on ahead, very quickly, and even in the state he was in he knew Milsi would be safe with Diomb and Bamba. He should not have spoken! It was cruel, degrading. It was unholy. Poor Thelda! He had loved Thelda, he had. They had had their quarrels, as who hadn't, but they had had a splendid life. And now she was gone, married to another man, and here he was, a wandering adventurer desperately trying to relive a part of his life that was dead.

He was not the same Seg Segutorio who had so happily marched through the Hostile Territories, all those seasons ago, with Thelda, and with his old dom and Delia. No. He was different now.

He'd been a great noble, lording it over rich lands, and he'd lost all that because he'd tried to outlaw slavery. He'd told kings and emperors what they could do. He'd commanded armies in battle. And now he had found a woman in his life for whom he could cherish a great and genuine affection, who might turn back the years for him, cause the clepsydra's water to run back up into the upper vessel. . . .

Milsi wouldn't so confidently, meaning the best, have slapped a harsh cistern-cleaning poultice on the wound in his old dom's chest . . . Poor Thelda! She was gone. He no longer loved the woman who was Thelda and who was married to Lol Polisto. He recalled the love he had felt for the Thelda of long ago, when they'd marched through the Hostile Territories, when they'd struggled for an empire.

No. It was so.

He could find it in his heart to love this Milsi, for all the oddness he sensed about her history. He had not so much found in her a new meaning to life, as a new reason to live a proper life once again.

As to her feelings for him, they remained obscure, despite that he felt she had been shafted with him by the same bolt of lightning. It was entirely possible when they returned to civilization and her home she would give him a cool "thank you" and then turn away and forget him.

Well, so be it, by Vox! He knew what he wanted, now. So, if that was how the adventure turned out, he'd use what skill and cunning he had to alter that outcome . . .

All that had happened was gone. It was smoke blown with the wind.

"By Beng Dikkane!" he said, calling on the patron saint of all the ale-drinkers of Paz. "I could do with a wet right now!"

Following on, Diomb kept up a stream of questions.

"What is vosk? What are momolams? What is ponhso? What is dopa?"

Half-laughing, Milsi explained carefully. She was mindful of the responsibilities she had taken on with her acceptance of the two dinkus as companions.

Seg could not fail to notice the way in which she handled them, easy and yet with a quiet manipulation she must have learned as a lady in waiting to a queen.

Bamba chattered as much as Diomb.

"What is a spinning wheel? What are carts?"

And Diomb: "What is a ship?"

Seg slowed, ears cocked, listening.

Milsi showed no hesitation in her reply. She spoke with the same sure conviction anyone would use explaining what a cart was.

"Oh, a ship is a very large boat, and I have told you that a boat floats on water and carries people and things. Ships travel far over the seas, driven by the winds of heaven, and bring strange and exotic merchandise back home."

Walking on, Seg reflected that Milsi knew much and spoke warmly of ships. Here, in the midst of a jungle with a river, a great river, to be sure, as her only source of information? She could have learned this from books. But, from the way she spoke, Seg was convinced she had seen what she so vividly described, had seen the armadas of sail ploughing the shining seas, venturing to the corners of the world, sailing home again, argosies of treasure.

If his honorable intentions toward her were ever to be realized there was much, a very great deal, he must learn about her history. Then he laughed to himself in his old reckless raffish way. By the Veiled Froyvil! What did her history matter to him? He would do what he would do, and play his part manfully, and if Erthyr the Bow smiled on him he would win what his heart desired.

# CHAPTER SIX

## Milsi causes more aggravation

They reached the Kazzchun River in good order and turned north along the bank. The brown water slid past and upon its still amiable flow the keels of commerce passed up and down. There were still plenty of sails to be seen, for Milsi said the head of navigation lay far upriver, and beyond that the paddle driven barks penetrated for many more dwaburs yet.

They entered the first township with due caution, although Milsi insisted that strangers would receive the need that was their due.

"A hulking great Bowman warrior, and two dinkus from the forest may attract unwelcome attention," she said, with that tiny dint between her delectable eyebrows. "But a few cheerful words, and perhaps a small offering to the local godling in his temple, should smooth the way."

"I trust so," said Seg. "Although the local godling's temple I am most in need of is to be found in the nearest tavern."

"I shall begin to believe you are a drunkard, Seg Segutorio!"

"Not so, my lady. Just that a fellow needs to wash away the dust from his throat from time to time."

"We shall see."

The place was called Lasindle, small and run-down, with wooden airy houses roofed with the leaves of papishin that were commonly used for this purpose in many parts of Kregen. Neither Seg nor Milsi felt any surprise that places in the world separated by vast distances should grow the same kinds of plants and harbor the same kinds of animals. That was perfectly natural to them. There were plenty of strange and weird plants and animals to be found inhabiting selected portions of the world to make those found universally to pass without comment.

The local godling was a fish-tailed lady called Kazzchun-faril and her temple lifted above the houses, and its walls were of wood lavishly carved and decorated. The papishin-leaved roof covered a goodly area of cells and secret places. Milsi and the others went into the outer court and the sight of two gold croxes made the priestess's eyes light up with avarice.

"May the great and glorious fishiness of Kazz-chun-faril light upon you and your hooks never be drawn empty," intoned a lady in a swathing robe of fish-scales, and tawdry bangles. "Go with the goddess's blessing."

So, with that out of the way, they went across the muddy square to The Hook and Net. Here a few copper coins produced the local brew. Without proper corn or vines, the locals produced their liquor from the bounty of the forest. Seg sipped. He made a face.

"I judge Diomb and Bamba will never touch a drop of the good stuff if this ruins their palates," he said.

Diomb sipped, spluttered and looked affronted.

Bamba sipped, sipped again, looked at Milsi, smiled, and finished the jug.

"H'm, young lady. I shall not carry you to bed."

The delights of roast ponsho were available, for meat animals were carried downstream from the enormous pastures farther north. Momolams, those small, yellow tubers of the delicious taste, complemented roast ponsho. Also, there were local dishes, mostly of fish cooked in an amazing variety of ways. The bread, baked from flour brought down the river, was gritty and coarse and would wear a person's teeth out well within two hundred years.

The two dinkus lapped up everything new with an appetite at once greedy and charming.

From the caverns of the Coup Blag Seg had brought his pouch-full of gold coins. He used these sparingly. He noticed that Milsi, also, had a pouch of coins, and he surmised that these had come from the same source as his own, or, perhaps, were leftovers of those she would habitually carry as handmaid to the queen.

When the reckoning was paid, and the word was mentioned, Diomb said, "What is money?"

"Ah, now," said Seg, wisely, scratching his nose. "Now there you pose a question that has bedeviled men and women for thousands of seasons. Money! If we did not need it, why, then—"

"We have none in the forest," pointed out Bamba.

"I will tell you this. Money is hard to obtain and easy to lose. With it you can buy—that is, get hold of—many things. But if you think only of money, you're done for."

Milsi gave a more reasoned explanation, so that the dinkus, naturally, said: "Then how will we obtain this money if it is necessary to live in the outside world?"

"Work."

"What is work?"

As Milsi explained Seg looked out of the window. He pointed to the three stakes set up side by side against the larger house with mud cladding to its wooden walls. Each stake was crowned with a human head. Two were men, one was female; two were Fristles, one was an Och.

"See those heads out there? They are there because their owners instead of working stole goods or money from other honest folk."

Milsi said: "Oh, Seg—the penalty here for thievery is to have the hand cut off. I don't think—"

Seg looked meaningfully upon the two dinkus.

"And the hands cut off!"

Then, sotto voce to Milsi, "I don't want them up to their usual common-possession habits. If we scare 'em enough they won't get into trouble."

"Yes, well. I suppose you are right."

Bamba and Diomb were suitably impressed.

"The outside world is indeed a strange place. Far more strange than ever the elders told us."

"There is," said Seg, helpfully, "a whole lot more."

A movement in the mud square took his attention.

He pointed again. "Look there! See that fellow with the yellow skin and the blue pigtail? His hair hanging down like a rope, like a twisted vine?"

They all looked out. The small coffle of slaves, trudging from the large mud-walled house, were in a poor state. The fellow Seg pointed out with the shaven yellow skull and the blue pigtail had tusks reaching up each side of his jaw. His eyes were bloodshot. His body was robustly strong and fit, endowed with muscle.

"It is uncommon strange to see a Chulik as slave. They are mercenaries, fighting men trained up from birth. They are first-class warriors and they are not cheap to hire. I wonder what he did to get himself in this fix?"

Chained before the Chulik a little Och slumped along, his six limbs giving him some assistance, for Ochs, although only around four feet tall, use their middle limbs as hands or feet as circumstances dictate. His puffy face and lemon-shaped head looked thoroughly hangdog.

Following the Chulik a beaked Rapa, hawklike in appearance, his orange and blue feathers bedraggled, stumped along, careful not to drag the bight of chain tight.

Other diffs and apims trudged along in the miserable slave column, and the Katakis lashed them with thick whips, or buffetted them with the flats of the steel strapped to their tails.

"If they don't cut off your hands and head," said Seg, heavily, "they'll take you up as slaves. So—do not take anything that is not yours. That is stealing."

"We will remember," said Diomb, most chastened.

The pygmies aroused considerable interest in the fisherfolk of Lasindle. A group of them in the opposite window corner kept shooting looks toward Diomb and Bamba. They were mostly apims, not all, and Seg began to feel a stuffiness in the atmosphere. He just hoped that he would not have to become embroiled in some stupid affray because these fishermen did not allow dinkus into their tavern. That kind of barbaric custom was known.

He also did not fail to miss the interest they took in the great longsword strapped to his back. He'd kept the sword because it belonged to the Bogandur. As for Seg himself, his old dom had shown him, often and often, how to wield the thing, and to hold it properly, and how to cut and thrust and cleave a path through the midst of a confused battle, as well as how to meet an opponent in single combat. Seg could handle the longsword; but it was not his chosen weapon. If he came to handstrokes he was most comfortable with the drexer scabbarded at his side, or a rapier and left-hand dagger.

All the same, he firmly believed in shafting his enemies before they got within striking range.

Uneasily, he said to Milsi: "I believe we should leave here very soon."

"Oh?"

"I'm not much enamored of the looks of those fishermen."

"But they are ordinary honest fisherfolk—"

"Oh, aye, indisputably. But they're like any honest folk in their tavern. They don't like strangers, particularly strangers they feel may wish them harm."

"That's nonsense! I don't see—"

"All the same, my lady, drink up and we will leave."

Just as they were about to quit The Hook and Net a rumble of coarse voices from the stoop heralded a couple of Katakis. They stamped their feet. They swished their bladed tails.

Seg stood aside.

Milsi sailed on, oblivious of the newcomers, making for the door.

With the two dinkus at his side, Seg watched, and it was all over in a twinkling.

Milsi quite expected to walk out of the doorway unimpeded and if anyone happened to be there, her manner made it perfectly plain, then they'd scuttle out of her way.

The Katakis did not scuttle.

They pushed in, and where in most races of Kregen people entering a tavern would be laughing and chattering, joyous in the delights to come, Katakis just marched in with their usual dour and grim absence of humor.

They pushed into Milsi.

Her surprise was genuine.

"You boors!" she cried, regaining her balance. "Do you not know to stand aside when a lady passes?"

They turned their vicious low-browed faces toward her. Their bladed tails flicked above their heads. Snaggle teeth showed as—in this situation— the Katakis could take their unhealthy dregs of amusement.

"Shishi! You speak overboldly—"

"Get out of my way, rasts!"

They did not like that. One put out a hand and

seized the Lady Milsi by her arm, and the other wrapped his tail about her waist.

"Ho! One for the coffle, this! A fine promising piece of merchandise."

Seg moved as a leaping leem moves. Feral, deadly, merciless.

His fist struck twice.

The two Katakis slumped to the floor, unconscious.

"Now let us get out of here, and right now! Come on you two—and, Diomb, stow that dratted blowpipe!"

Pelting out from the stoop they hit the square and ran like crazy down the first of the mazy alleyways. Seg headed for the river.

"Where are we going?" Milsi panted it out, running with her head up, her hips going from side to side; but running fleetly and well.

"River. Find a boat. The rains—are due soon. Now, woman—run!"

The dinkus kept up with fleet agility. Seg held his pace down. He would not leave them, and he could not leave Milsi, who had caused all this aggravation.

The rains would come pelting down soon, casting a pall of water over everything and turning the mud into a quagmire. He wanted to be well away into the river by then.

The waterside presented an appearance of lazy apathy. Fisherfolk were not working at his time, knowing the rains were due. The busiest activity centered on a long narrow canoe-like craft where the Kataki slavers they had seen crossing the square were herding the coffle aboard.

Diomb settled the whole thing.

He skidded to a halt. His blowpipe twitched up. "Dratted Katakis!" he said.

His cheeks puffed, the first dart sped.

Seg howled in frustration; but the damage was done.

He slapped up his bow, nocked an arrow, and Diomb had puffed a second dart. Two Katakis clapped hands to their necks above the rim of their harness, startled. They saw the pygmies, they started to jeer at them, and then they fell down.

Another took a clothyard shaft through his throat and a fourth yelped as a dart stung his lowering face. He, too, fell down shortly thereafter.

The fifth and six were punched clean through by arrows. The seventh tried to run and, ironically, the dart took him in the fleshy root of his tail. He ran on and could not stop and tumbled headlong into the water.

A furious splashing followed, and the crunch of jaws.

Seg roared up to the canoe-like craft, known as a schinkitree in these parts, and stared down on the slaves.

"Who is willing to paddle to freedom with me?"

"I!" and "I!"

"All right. You—" pointing at the Och, "find the keys. You—" with a fierce stab at the Chulik— "chuck the dratted Katakis into the river when we have the keys! *Bratch!*"

At that command the slaves bratched. They jumped.

The key was found, the clever fingers of the little Och released the first of the slaves on the chain, the Chulik, after a dour look at Seg, started hurling the Katakis into the river. Jaws crunched.

"Get aboard, all!" called Seg. "Hurry!"

The two dinkus even in this extremity of urgency assisted Milsi aboard, waiting for her. She went into the schinkitree with a regal step that looked most becoming. Seg pushed off. He stared back across the waterside to the first of the wooden houses.

From the ragged alleyway men were running out, apims, Katakis, Rapas, all yelling and waving weapons. He did not bother to shaft them. There had been no time to cut out his arrows, and he did not wish to waste any more. The boat was off from the riverside, surging out into midstream as the freed slaves took up the paddles and dug deep.

Then the rain slashed down.

A solid curtain of water hid the bank and the forest and the township.

The Chulik roared out: "By Likshu the Treacherous! I am free again! Downstream. Paddle downstream. We will make Mattamlad at the mouth of the river. I have friends there—"

Seg chopped him off brutally.

"I am in command here, Chulik. We paddle upstream. That is without question."

His bow, arrow nocked, aimed at the Chulik's breast.

"Apim yetch! I am Nath Chandarl! Nath the Dorvenhork!"

"That is as it may be. But, by the Veiled Froyvil, dom, we paddle upstream—unless you wish to become flint-fodder."

The Chulik started. He stared from those narrow eyes at Seg, saw the bow, heard what he said. He lowered his fist.

"You are a Bowman of Loh?"

"Yes."

"In that case—"

"Look, dom. They will expect us to paddle downstream. That is where they will search. We have a goodly craft, strong paddlers. We go upstream and they'll never find us. Later, when we have made our fortunes, we may return downstream and you can rejoin your friends."

"That does, by Likshu the Treacherous, make sense, apim."

The current, lazy though it might still be here, was carrying them downstream. Seg, without taking his gaze or the aim of the shaft from the Chulik, Nath the Dorvenhork, said with a harsh emphasis: "Paddle, doms. Paddle upstream and let us lose ourselves in the rain."

"Yes," shrilled the Och, wildly. "As sure as my name is Umtig the Lock, the apim speaks sooth!"

Once more the paddles bit. This time the boat turned and headed upstream. The paddlers, slaves only moments before, drew their blades through the brown water with strong and determined sweeps. They had been slave; now they were free. Not one of them would voluntarily return to slavery. They would paddle and paddle, strive and battle, to avoid that ghastly fate.

Slowly, Seg lowered his bow. This Chulik, by his sobriquet of Dorvenhork, was a bowman also. With Seg's movement from the stern of the schinkitree the Chulik relaxed. Merciless, ruthless, like all his race, he had recognized another master bowman, and, also, seen the wisdom of the decision to paddle upstream. He took up a paddle and joined in the rhythmic swing and stroke of the other ex-slaves.

In the stern, with Milsi, Diomb and Bamba, Seg surveyed his new command. They were veiled in the gray and silver rain. The brown river gurgled past below.

Whatever the future might hold, they were on their way to it right now. . . .

# CHAPTER SEVEN

## Stranded

A sennight later and well up the river the fugitives found it expedient to make a camp for a few days on one of the islands dotting the Kazzchun River hereabouts. The river rolled along, redolent of brown mud and damp growing things, choked with wildfowl, the mudflats always shimmering with the flash of wings. The denizens of the water fought and thrived, and, all in all, there was food a plenty.

The histories of the freed slaves were interesting and shared a common thread. Folk who are born to slavery are born to slavery, as the saying went. Others, caught in petty crimes, found themselves chained and trudging along in the coffle, punished enough and more for their sins.

The little Och, Umtig the Lock, more than once exclaimed when he spoke: "By Diproo the Nimble-Fingered!" By this men knew him to be a thief.

The Chulik had formed an odd kind of respect for Seg. He had asked to inspect the Lohvian longbow, and made a stupid mewling whistle of admiration as he bent it.

"I am used to the dorven bow, the crossbow, or even the weak flat bow; this round longbow is indeed a marvel."

Seg had never had much time for Chuliks. Raised from birth as they were to be mercenaries, and highly paid ones at that, they knew little of humanity. They were ruthless in their exactment of debts. But, in these latter days, he found that human converse was possible with specimens of the race. He simply handled each eventuality as it arose, and felt distinct relief that Nath the Dorven-hork had desisted from that first desire to shaft him.

Diomb brought up an interesting question, that made Seg roar with laughter, and then sober, and then—lamely—try to explain.

"You stole this boat, Seg. You are a thief. They will cut off your hands, and your head—"

"They have to catch me first."

"Yes—but, you said—"

"I know, Diomb, and mark me! What I said was right. But you saw the situation. All honest men abhor Katakis as slavers, even though they condone slavery. Katakis are anti-human in a way that—" Here Seg looked around the campsite on the river island. The Chulik was nowhere in sight. "—in a way even that Chuliks are not. But I do not seek to pretend I did not steal the boat or that stealing is a crime. Just, that—"

"Thievery is an honest profession like any other!" protested the Och, Umtig the Lock, most heated.

"There are degrees, dom, and well you know it."

They wrangled amicably for a space, and then Seg said to Umtig: "And mind you do not lead Diomb into bad habits, you rogue. I cherish your outlook in some things, not all."

The traffic on the river thinned past the last town through which they had paddled at dead of night. Local produce traveled up and down, and the massive rafts carried stone and building materials to the south, as the slender schinkitrees carried wood upstream to the great plains.

"Let us paddle out and seize one of these craft laden with treasure, slit all their throats, and take the gold!" counseled a hulking great apim called Ortyg the Undlefar.

"We are not pirates, not renders!" said Seg, shocked at the uncouthness of it all.

"Why not? We have a boat, we have fighting men, we have—"

"And we have no weapons, apart from those of the four who rescued us," said a Fristle, Naghan the Slippy.

"We descend on them unheard and unseen! We will soon have weapons!" Ortyg the Undlefar showed his contempt for those who did not understand the render's trade.

A Syblie, a girl with the delectable body of a mature woman and the face of an innocent child in the way of her race of diffs, spoke up. "I would like to go home."

Others took up this call. A lath-thin apim, known as Hundle the Design, said: "I agree we would like to go home. But I, for one, would prefer to return with a pocket full of gold. But, doms, I would not like to gain the gold through piracy or thievery."

A Khibil whose haughty, fox-featured face showed that like all Khibils, he considered himself a cut above everyone else—known as Khardun the Franch, said in his lofty way: "I am a hyr-paktun. Let us find a great lord and hire out our services as fighting men. We will soon make our fortunes."

A mild-mannered Relt stylor, Caphlander the Quill, ventured to say that not all present had the skills of mercenary fighting men, paktuns.

Seg felt the twinge hearing that name. There had been just such a mild-mannered Relt when he'd first met his old dom, far and far away from here, and that Relt's name had been Caphlander. Relts were distant cousins of the ferocious Rapas, and usually they were employed as domestics, stylors, clerical help, accountants.

"We stick together," Seg declared. "We are going to reach the town of Mewsansmot. After that, with full bellies, you may go your own separate ways. There may also be gold in it, too." He cocked a cautious eye at Milsi.

She took the point at once.

"I believe there will be gold for all of you if you help to bring us safely to Mewsansmot."

The only serious opposition to this plan came from the hulking apim, Ortyg the Undlefar. Seg told him that he was at perfect liberty to leave the party. He would be put onto the riverbank of his choosing and from thence go where he willed. Ortyg chilled considerably in his own plans and oppositions to others after that.

The plain fact was that these one-time slaves had been taken up for a variety of reasons. Ortyg, now, was a real villain. The beautiful Syblie was a slave because members of her race were usually slaves. She had been there to be sold to a new master. Some were petty criminals, some were debtors, some had been snatched from their homes.

Seg sorted them out in his mind, allotting them places in his table of possible uses.

He took the opportunity to have a word with the Khibil, Khardun the Franch.

"I salute you, Khardun, as a hyrpaktun. How is it, if you care to tell me, that you became slave?"

Seg knew how to handle Khibils. So long as they believed they were the greatest, then things ran smoothly.

"How I became slave, dom? I will tell you. I am a hyrpaktun, I am a mercenary who hires out only for top rates, who commands, who orders. I served King Crox well. I had a detachment to take downriver, and this I did. When I returned, the king had gone to some heathenish place called the Coup Blag. The lady Mab, who was married to him in a ceremony, so I am told, of the utmost shortness, followed. The Kov Llipton—"

"Ah!" said Seg. "Now I have heard of him. He is the regent, is he not, and rules in the king's place?"

"That is so. I do not know how I offended him. But whatever I did, it was wrong, and I was stripped, my pakzhan taken from me, my sword broken, and I was shipped out as slave." Here the Khibil's savage and resentful look did not surprise Seg. The pakzhan, a golden head of a zhantil, perhaps the most splendid of all Kregen's wild animals that he knew of, strung on a silken thread and looped in a top buttonhole or over a shoulder knot, was the highest award conferred by hyrpaktuns upon members of their trade. It was hard to come by. A pakzhan glittering gold at the throat of a hyrpaktun marked him as a soldier of fortune of the highest renown.

Seg did not think it opportune to mention that he, too, had won the pakzhan and was a hyrpaktun. He had been a noble lord long enough for his more reckless days as a mercenary warrior to recede into the past for him.

"Tell me of Kov Llipton."

"He is like any other great lord, I suppose. He runs the country now. I think that he was mightily displeased that Queen Mab followed the king to the Coup Blag."

Ah! said Seg to himself. That did not take a deal of worming out. If this Llipton fellow wanted to be king, and King Crox dead, then he'd have to marry the queen.

"You saw Queen Mab?"

"No. She came from Jholaix—"

"From Jholaix!"

"Aye, Seg. She brought a dowry of wine so splendid that, well, I swear it was enough to make all of the kingdom drunk for three seasons."

"And no hangovers."

"No. Never! Not with the wines of Jholaix!"

They paddled upriver. No one of the passing craft offered to molest them. Milsi judged that pursuit had, indeed, hared off downriver.

Diomb came up to Seg as they paddled past one of the many islands dotting the broad river here, and said: "I am astonished by what that girl, the Syblie Malindi, says. She wants to go home. That is understandable. But, by Clomb of the Ompion Never-Miss! If she does that she will be slave again. That is what home means to her."

"There are different sorts of slaves, Diomb. Oh, some folk who keep slaves treat them well, almost as part of the family. Syblies and Relts aspire to that condition. It is in the fields, the mines, the terrible places where men and women work until they drop, that slavery at its worst may be found."

"And, another thing. There are mercenaries, paktuns, among us. They take—money—from other people to fight for them. That is, indeed, most strange."

Seg laughed.

"If I do not like fighting and do not wish to risk my precious skin in a battle, then I will pay someone else to go out and fight for me. It is simple."

"Well, I suppose so. But all mercenaries are not paktuns—"

"No. A paktun is a mercenary who has gained some fame. A hyrpaktun is a most famous paktun. Yet lots of mercenaries are dubbed paktuns these days. The custom is new. Just about only the young ones, the coys, are not called paktuns in general usage these days."

"Well," said Diomb. "I think that if I have to work to gain this money, then I will be a paktun."

Seg was not surprised.

"You could. You would do well with your dratted blowpipe—your ompion. That would tickle 'em up on a battlefield, by the Veiled Froyvil, yes!"

The Chulik, Nath the Dorvenhork, in the general way of Chuliks, did not laugh or smile when he made his comment. But for a Chulik it was revealing enough.

"I agree. The little fellow would earn his hire!"

There was, Seg could see, a strange kind of brotherhood developing between the exponents of missile weapons.

He'd always been a feckless sort of scamp and so he'd never thought overmuch of the way he ought to treat diffs. Diffs were diffs; that was all there was to it. In these later seasons he had seen a deal of the world and had picked up new ways of handling exceptional members of odd races. But he'd never bothered his head much over Chuliks; they went their cold, mercenary way, and he went his.

Still, if the Dorvenhork wanted to secure allies, that would be no bad thing.

The political map had changed with the coming of age of King Crox, and he now controlled the length of the river from past Mewsansmot in the north to a new shanty town he'd erected ten or so dwaburs from the coast. King Crox did not control the mouth of the river and Mattamlad. But, then, it was highly unlikely that King Crox controlled anything at all in the fabulous world of Kregen, being no doubt stuffed down in the intestines of some horrendous monster in the maze of the Coup Blag.

A little Ift, Twober the So, went past with a long look at Seg's bow. Twober's ears stuck up in two shapely points almost past the crown of his head. His eyebrows slanted up, and his eyes slanted up. Woodsfolk, the Ifts, not jungle folk, and Twober had wandered down here to South Pandahem from his home over the massive central mountains in North Pandahem.

Various plans were discussed by groups of the escaped slaves. All well understood their peril, and the punishments that would be their lot if they

were recaptured. Any slave-owning society is hard
on runaways.

Ortyg the Undlefar, although chastened, kept on
a monotonous series of suggestions. All boiled
down to paddling out and capturing a rich merchant raft, boat or schinkitree, massacring all the
occupants, and disappearing with the gold and
jewels.

The evening light, all a glorious mingling of
jade and ruby, threw mazy shadows upon the sliding water. Waterfowl sprawled on the mudflats or
turned in a glinting pinioned array in the last flights
before nightfall. The two second Moons of Kregen
were due early tonight, the Twins would cast
down a pinkish radiance that would light up the
world in a strange and ghostly reflection of the
twin suns, Zim and Genodras. The warm muddy
scents rose.

The fires were set well back from the banks of
the island in secure places so as not to be observed
by craft passing along the river. Food there was in
plenty. Palines grew in lush profusion. A slothful-
ness could easily overtake these people but for the
ever-present fear of discovery and the terrors that
would follow.

Guards were set. Diomb and Bamba disappeared
farther back into the interior of the island where
the vegetation, although it might not rival in any
way the riot of the jungle, gave them a sense of
home. Seg settled down, with Milsi and the Syblie
girl, Malindi, sleeping not too far off and within
call. He placed the Bogandur's long sword at his
side, with his own Lohvian longbow. The drexer
he placed near to his right hand as he slept.

He had the last watch and would be called when

Kregen's fourth moon, She of the Veils, rose four glasses before dawn.

With the habits of a lifetime he awoke a few moments before he expected to be called. He yawned and stretched. He'd never wondered over much about the oddity of his own body, which must have some kind of blood-filled clepsydra somewhere inside. He and the Bogandur were old campaigners in matters of this nature.

He stood up and went toward the bank with its screen of bushes where the lookout was kept expecting to find Rafikhan, the Rapa with the orange and blue feathers, just setting off to wake him.

Perhaps he was a little early. The Twins were wheeling away to the west and the new roseate-golden tinge flushing the eastern sky was She of the Veils about to pour her glory upon the face of the world. He reached the lookout post without meeting a soul.

Rafikhan was just sitting up holding his head.

About to let fly with a torrent of abuse, Seg paused. Between the Rapa's fingers a dark liquid thread shone greasily, staining down his facial feathers.

"Rafikhan! What's amiss?"

The Rapa hissed his pain, rocking backwards and forwards. Beside him the body of the little Ift, Twober the So, lay in an ungainly and lax posture. Seg bent.

Twober was dead, his skull bashed in. The blow that had killed him had been delivered with the same force as the blow that had knocked Rafikhan unconscious.

Instantly, Seg looked to the bank.

The boat was gone.

So he knew it all.

The camp roused out and Seg silenced their babble.

He counted heads.

Almost half of the ex-slaves were no longer present.

"May Likshu the Treacherous draw forth his entrails to be devoured by worms!" declared Nath the Dorvenhork.

"By Rhapaporgolam the Reiver of Souls!" Rafikhan's voice hissed in the moons' light. "The cramph hit me shrewdly."

No need to ask who had struck the Rapa and slain the Ift.

"Ortyg the Undlefar!" said Milsi. "He has persuaded many poor deluded souls to follow him—"

"And he has taken our boat!"

"We are stranded here, abandoned on this little island . . ."

Stranded they were, isolated on their mound of mud in a river boiling with hungry bellies and ravenous jaws.

# CHAPTER EIGHT

## Of the sharing of clothes

"Now what are we going to do?"

Hundle the Design, skinny as a spear-shaft, stepped forward. Everyone left in the party gathered around as the twin suns rose. Their warmth on this morning, their refulgence, brought no happy welcome.

Hundle had proved knowledgeable about the boat and the way she should be handled. Now he said: "I was a schinkitree master before my boat hit a half-submerged log and filled and sank. I lost my boat, all the merchandise I carried for the merchant Dorlan Merlo, who was a Lamnia and my friend, my living and my freedom."

They all listened, not shouting out about what the hell had this to do with their plight now. The thin ex-boat master was clearly leading up to something important he had to say.

"Go on, Hundle the Design," said Milsi.

"The king, since he took full command of the river, has swept the whole length he controls free of pirates. The renders were trapped, caught, slain. This poor deluded fool, Ortyg the Undlefar, will surely come to grief. As Pandrite is my witness, this will happen.''

"Yes," said Milsi. "I judged him by his talk of renders not to understand."

"He and I," said the Chulik Nath Chandarl, stroking one of his tusks with a thumb, "were dragged upriver together. I think my friends in Mattamlad and his were on opposite sides of the law."

By this, Seg gathered that the idiot Ortyg had probably been a pirate out along the coast of Pandahem and among the islands of the Koroles.

He said, "I thank you for your information, horter Hundle. This means, I take it, that that onker Ortyg will be taken up and beheaded. But, also, that we may signal to a passing craft and hope to be taken off?"

"Yes, horter Seg. They will rescue us, for that is the way of the Kazzchun River. They will, of course, charge for their services."

"Oh, of course."

A wailing started up at this news.

They all cried out in various ways, and it summed up as: "But we are all naked and have no money. We are clearly slaves!"

"Shastum! Silence!" yelled Seg.

He quieted them down, and then went on: "I have a little gold. I think it will pay our passage to the nearest town. The vexatious question is, how are we to become honest horters and horteras, and no longer slaves?"

Milsi said: "Good master Hundle. Is it not possible for us to have been in a boat that sank? We would have lost all in the accident.''

Quite calmly, Milsi took off her blue tunic. It was badly ripped, and she held it up high. Looking at her, clad only in a tiny blue loincloth, Seg caught his breath.

"This tunic will make loincloths for a number of us, and horter Seg can spare some of his scarlet breechclout. We will look decent enough when we are rescued.''

Shyly, Malindi said: "I would love to have a loincloth of that beautiful blue, mistress.''

"And you shall be my new handmaiden, Malindi, I promise you.''

It was said so naturally, so unaffectedly, that Seg barely noticed. He could not keep on looking at Milsi like this, and had to turn away, and found he could not.

"Well, Seg the Horkandur! And where is your knife? And your breechclout!''

With the aid of his knife the women of the party fashioned just-respectable loincloths for themselves and almost enough breechclouts for the men—drawn tightly!

Diomb and Bamba wanted to know what all the fuss was about. It fell to Seg to stumble over an explanation that slaves were expected to be naked or wear the gray slave breechclout, but that horters and horteras, ladies and gentlemen, usually covered themselves up.

"Then it is a sign of this rank you have tried to explain?''

"More or less—''

"The outside world becomes stranger and stranger the more one learns,'' declared Bamba, giving her bark apron a flick. "I will willingly wear nothing at all most of the time, and anyone is welcome to share a piece of my bark."

Somebody listening laughed. Somehow that broke the fearful tension that gripped the less hardy of the ex-slaves and seemed a good augury for the future. Seg was interested to notice the people Ortyg the Undlefar had failed to impress into his schemes: The Khibil was too proud, the Chulik a highly qualified and paid paktun, the Rapa just not interested, even the little Och thief was not into the red-roaring blood-letting of piracy. The Fristle was not happy in a boat at the best of times, and as for the others, for the best of reasons they had refused to join the render's trade.

All in all, decided Seg, he had a likely bunch with him now, apart from the timid ones who would no doubt do as they were told. If bluff could succeed, they stood every chance of success.

Diomb in his perennially inquisitive way brought up an interesting point. He was puzzled. If, he wanted to know, slaves were property, and the slave owners very hard on runaways, then surely they'd chase after the people here and re-take them?

Milsi took it upon herself to explain that these people had not been personally owned slaves. They had been merchandise in the hands of Katakis, slave-traders, and would be regarded as stock. Anyway, many of the Kataki owners had been killed. No authority acting on behalf of an owner whose slave had run off would be involved. Seg listened, and realized that a great deal of the apathy he had noticed before caused by the absence of King Crox was at work here. He felt pretty sure that the Katakis themselves should they ever run across these people and recognize them would act with harshness.

Nath the Dorvenhork and Khardun the Franch, when the skimpy loincloths had been handed out and adjusted, approached Seg. With all the circumlocution and formality of warriors requesting the loan of another warrior's weapon—the Kregish rituals extended in labyrinthine protocol for these occasions—they asked to borrow Seg's knife. They intended to cut stout staves from the woods, and sharpen the ends in the fire and thus fashion spears for themselves.

"Just," said the Dorvenhork. "In case."

"Right gladly, doms," said Seg cheerfully, and he tossed his knife into the air. Neither attempted to beat the other to the catch and the knife went splut into the earth. Seg laughed—but to himself. Khibil and Chulik; there'd be a constant game of seizing the advantage between these two—and not in petty ways, either, by Vox . . .

The stranded party took considerable interest and delight in the antics of the little Och, Umtig the Lock. He fashioned a long rope of twisted vines, with a loop at each end, and with this whistling around his head he trotted off into the island forest.

The land sloped gently up from the coast to the interior mountains, but the slope was enough to create a varied biosphere. The rain forest that Seg usually thought of as jungle, gave place to cloud forest. The dwarf forest farther on extended for only a short distance between the cloud forest and the plains. Umtig the lock trotted confidently on, whirling his plaited rope of vines.

Here he expected to find a particular species of

monkey among the denizens of the trees, the humming birds, the fighting wasps, the horned lizards and all the splendid and various forms of life flourishing each in its own niche.

Chulik and Khibil watched the Och depart, and then turned to the grave matter of who should pick up Seg's knife.

Seg settled all that nonsense.

"If you two are going to cut spears, it would be a good idea if you'd go off now and keep an eye on Umtig."

They jerked as though stung. Then the Dorvenhork said, "You may take the knife, horter Khardun."

"I will carry it, Nath Chandarl; you may use it first."

"As you wish. The Och is almost out of sight."

They followed on with the swift stalking gait of the fighting man. Umtig went about his task with perfect confidence. He peered about most carefully up into the trees. Presently he uttered a little Och exclamation of delight, and whirled the vine rope with deft precision.

The loop spun up into the air. Umtig jerked the line. With a swooshing rush a bundle of multi-colored fur tumbled down. Umtig caught the little monkey with a cry of delight.

"This is a spinlikl," he said, and at once set to crooning and making baby-mewing sounds to caress the monkey to quietude. The small creature wriggled and struggled, his eight limbs swishing about, and then he quieted down. His body was no larger than a fair-sized melon, and his eight limbs each stretched out farther than a man's full arm-reach. Each limb had a fully formed hand, lithe-

fingered, deft, powerful, with sharp nails. The
spinlikl made no sound, but squirmed against
Umtig's chest and settled himself comfortably, three
or four arms wrapped about the Och's neck, the
rest wrapped about his upper body.

Umtig beamed his pleasure.

The Chulik and the Khibil looked on, waiting
for the Och to return to the main party, then they
set about cutting staves with which to fashion
spears.

Umtig, returning in his personal triumph to the
camp, ripped a paline branch free from a handy
bush and began feeding a steady stream of the
berries to the spinlikl. These sweet yellow cherry-
like fruits found growing over most parts of Kregen
proved a source of constant delight, a sovereign
remedy for a hangover, a necessity with which to
conclude a meal, a digestive of the first order, a
boon to all humankind.

"My supremely clever spinlikl," Umtig said to
Seg. "I will soon have him trained into the verita-
ble paradigm of invisible deftness. I shall call him
Lord Clinglin."

Milsi smiled. "I had a little mili-milu once who
was called Pantor Fotaix. How we silly humans
love to give our pets grand titles!"

Such was the good humor of the party now that
they had clothes of a sort, the promise of money
and every chance of rescue, no one appeared to
express any high-minded and respectable abomination of Umtig's new pet. For, of course, he was no
ordinary household pet to be loved and adored and
played with. He was a most adept adjunct in the
trade dedicated to and cared for by Diproo the
Nimble-fingered.

When all was declared ready they watched for a suitable craft passing up the river. Still no one wished to chance descending the Kazzchun River, Despite the general belief the Katakis would write off the lost merchandise and look for more. By the time they reached Lasindle they should be dressed properly and able to escape instant detection as escaped slaves. . . . But . . .

"There!" said Milsi with great confidence, pointing. "Set the fire."

The craft to which she pointed paddled along with forty paddles aside going in and out and up and down with perfect rhythm. Her after parts carried a covered-in cabin from which flags flew.

Hundle the Design tossed a brand into the pile of stump and twigs, of leaves and greenery and soon the smoke lifted, thick and coiling, and only slightly blown by the tiny breeze. Everyone jumped up and down and waved.

No one really believed the ornately large schinki-tree would paddle grandly past and leave them. No one really believed that . . . But . . . The moments passed with excruciating agony before, at last, the bows turned and the boat became a fore-shortened spear aimed at them with her paddles churning either side. The flags flew and the foam spurted and she came churning up to their little mud bank.

Very few people ever leaped into the water to drag a boat up onto the bank in the River of Bloody Jaws. Most boats possessed a small laddered ramp, something like a corvus, which ran out and provided a safe way to shore. The anchors were often merely large stones pierced with a hole for the chains or ropes. This vessel ran her gangway

out and the spiked end went thunk into the mud,
and men marched down, alert and watchful.

"What?" said Milsi, suddenly. "What does this
mean?"

For the men were armed and carried weapons,
and they fanned out as they touched the shore and
presented a formidable front. There were ten of
them, and they looked rough and tough, paktuns
with blue and yellow feathers in their helmets.
Then a wispy Xaffer walked ashore, his blue robes
trailing, his dreamy face giving him the look of a
man who lived in a private fantasy world of his
own. He carried a scrip, and his right temple was
ink-stained.

"Forgive the welcome," he said, holding up his
hand in greeting. "I give you the Llahal. But there
have been reports of pirates on the river."

"That Pandrite-forsaken Ortyg," someone to the
rear of the party said with great venom.

Hundle the Design stepped forward and as the
most experienced traveler among them upon the
river explained their situation. His story sounded
convincing. They were travelers whose craft had
sunk. Seg felt a vicious anger at the explanation of
the absence of paddlers, but he kept a calm face.
Now was not the time. The paddlers, being slaves,
and being chained to their benches, had, of course,
sunk with the boat . . .

Not all of them had reached this island. This
handful were the only survivors. Seg agreed with
that. They wanted nothing to do with the depreda-
tions of Ortyg the Undlefar and his band of
cutthroats.

"You are fortunate indeed to have survived the

jaws of the river. My master will be interested in your story. You are welcome to come aboard.''

They all carefully observed the fantamyrrh as they stepped into the boat. Long and narrow, with her paddlers chained to their benches at each side, she offered only adequate accommodation right aft where the master lived in state, and right forrard where the paktun guards were quartered. The rescued folk could, for the journey, sleep upon the central gangway. There were no masts. Along the gangway prowled the Whip-Deldars ensuring that the paddlers kept time and rhythm and dug deeply with all their strength.

The master turned out to be a jolly, perspiring, multi-chinned apim called Obolya Metromin. As a merchant specializing in the buying and selling of saddle animals, he liked to be called Obolya the Zorcanim. This was, to Seg, pitching it a little high; but he was in no case to argue the finer points of nomenclature.

Obolya sat upon a handsome chair, strewn with expensive silks and furs, beaming away upon the new arrivals. At his back his pavilion-like cabin rose, the flags fluttering. His personal guards flanked him, distinct from the boat-guards. Two charming girls saw to his needs, their pale bodies partially concealed by artfully draped gauzes, decorated with strings of pearls in the age-old custom. Obolya himself, in robes of some magnificence, exuded an air of benediction; but Seg was not the only one to see and realize that this fat, happy, charming man was a merchant of consummate shrewdness.

''Payment?'' he exclaimed, and held up a fat beringed hand in horror. ''Never could I exact payment for performing a good deed. Why, by

Pandrite the All-Powerful! Is it not the Law of the River to aid our unfortunate brothers and sisters? You will take wine, of course. I have a middling-fine Markable which clears the throat most effectively.''

So they all took wine.

This fine fat animal-trader was on his way upriver to buy what saddle-animals he could from traders out on the plains. Milsi looked at him carefully, and smiled, and intimated that if horter Obolya was going to Mewsansmot—

''Why, yes! I have business contacts there. All this is new to me, this is my first journey so far upriver. I trade normally in North Pandahem; but things political up there are parlous, most parlous. I am confident that if I can secure good cargoes of saddle animals I can sell every last one back in North Pandahem.''

Incautiously, Seg said: ''Then the journey around the island by sea is less dangerous than crossing the mountains?''

Obolya lowered his wine cup, of polished silver, studded with gems.

''Of course—as everyone knows. My business associate, a fine brave fellow, Naghan Loppelyer, just managed to stagger back home after an attempt to cross the mountains. He lost his caravan, his guards, his girls, his money, his clothes and escaped only with his life.''

''You are then from Tomboram?'' Milsi looked up.

''Yes. And a pretty pickle we are in up there, I can tell you.''

''Yes,'' said Milsi. Then, quickly, to Obolya: ''If you'd kindly take us to Mewsansmot I have friends there. I am sure I could arrange a number of profitable introductions.''

"My dear young lady! That is splendid! It is a bargain, as Pandrite is my witness!''

When he had the chance of a private word, Seg said to Milsi: "Look, my lady. You are the lady in waiting to the queen. Why don't we go straight to the capital? Surely your—''

"The king and queen are dead. We know that. The whole country is not sure, but suspects. I want to see my friends first, Seg. You'll just have to trust me in this.''

"Oh, I trust you all right. Perhaps you do not trust this Kov Llipton who is the regent?''

"I have no reason not to trust him. Anyway, he will do what he wants to do. I am only a hand-maiden.''

There was something else troubling Milsi, Seg could sense that with a sympathy that aroused his own guilt that he had not fully confided in her. Yes, they might have been shafted by the same bolt of lightning; but he felt sure that when Milsi did at last confide the more important parts of her history he would discover facts that, just perhaps, might better be left undiscovered.

He considered the interesting notion that she might be Queen Mab herself. He dismissed the idea because he and his old dom had seen the queen dead in the next cell to Milsi's. And it was certain the queen would be recognized somewhere along the river. If Queen Mab was Milsi and she trusted Kov Llipton—and, it seemed sure that so far there was no reason to distrust him apart from the cynical natures possessed by wandering pak-tuns—then there would be no need to continue with the masquerade. She could just sail grandly up to her palace in the capital city of Nalvinlad and take over from the regent.

Maybe, just maybe, if the handmaiden Milsi was really Queen Mab, she might not wish to marry Kov Llipton if that was his intention. She might have another in mind. If that was the case, Seg couldn't see that other fortunate man being a wandering warrior Bowman of Loh.

He brushed all this nonsense aside.

The facts were that the lady Milsi had asked him to be her jikai and to escort her safely to her friends in Mewsansmot.

This he intended to do to the best of his ability or die trying.

Milsi joined him as he sat on the central gangway trying to keep his stupid thoughts well away from the continuous hypnotic rhythm of the paddlers to either side, and, equally, away from the fantasy scenarios thronging his stupid old vosk skull of a head.

She wore a yellow blouse fastened with bone rosettes through loops of crimson thread. The blouse was almost a bolero jacket, its hem reaching to a point just above her navel. She still wore the scrap of blue loincloth. Her hair had been wound up and fastened with an overlarge stickpin whose head was fashioned into the likeness of a spinyfish, one of the delicacies of the river.

"Well, my Horkandur! You look mighty pensive!"

"Just wondering how all this will end."

"Do not fret. We are well on our way. Look at my new clothes. Obolya is most kind. Why don't you go aft and ransack his wardrobe?"

"Yes, yes, in a mur or two."

"You are grumpy, Seg!"

"I crave your pardon, my lady. It is just—just that—oh! I do not know! I know so little of you, and I was just puzzling if I wanted to know more. There. I'm honest with you."

She looked clearly at him, a long and level gaze to which he responded with his own fey blue gaze just as level and straight.

"Yes, Seg. I also have a family. A single child, not yet full grown. And I hunger to see her again!"

# CHAPTER NINE

## In which Seg hires on paktuns

The boat drew into the wooden piers of the wharfside in Nalvinlad. Many craft dotted the brown water, paddles flashed and the shouts of stentors as they guided their vessels joined in the clamor of birds above the fish quays. The slaves from Obolya's schinkitree were herded out, chained two and two, and taken off to the slave barracks for the night.

The city was not overlarge, girded with a stout wooden palisade strengthened with mudbrick. Here and there, particularly at the river gates and the few gates facing inland, the defenses were strengthened with blocks of masonry. Crowds surged about the business of a city, yet as he went ashore Seg noticed that same apathy that afflicted all the folk of the river since the disappearance of their king.

The palace, built of wood and mud brick, was encircled by its own separate stone wall. The cost of that must have been enormous. King Crox, since he came of age, had bustled about and transformed his kingdom, extending its boundaries up and down the river. He had done nothing about any lateral extension. Kingdoms in this part of South Pandahem stretched along rivers. They were, as Seg put it, as wide as you could reach with your outspread arms, and as long as you could fight your way and win and take territory.

King Crox, already given the name of the gold piece in customary use around here, had changed the name of his new kingdom. When he'd ascended the throne the realm had been called Nalvindrin. His conquests enlarged his domains enough for him to call the whole lot Croxdrin.

When the bandits from the Snarly Hills had caused interruption in the regular flow of commerce along his river, King Crox had taken his expedition in to quell them for good.

Already he had put down piracy on the river, now he wasn't going to stand still for a miserable bunch of drikingers. Well, he'd run into far more than he could handle in the Coup Blag. Still, the regent carried on the good work of keeping the river free from pirates.

Seg and the folk rescued with him stood by the Peral Gate and looked up.

A row of stakes lifted into the brilliance of the suns' radiance.

Each stake was crowned with a head.

"There's Ortyg the Undlefar," said Khardun, scornfully.

"And there and there!" exclaimed others, staring up and recognizing the heads of the people who had escaped with them and who had gone off on the render's trail with Ortyg.

"Kov Llipton moves fast" said Obolya, comfortably. "The moment these rasts were taken, swift boats flew up and down the river, warning us. That is why I hired on extra guards."

"The danger is over, I would think," said Milsi.

"Probably, my lady Milsi. But I will check with the authorities first, before I discharge my brave paktuns."

Khardun turned with his supercilious Khibil nose high.

"That is bad news for me, then, horter Obolya."

"Do not rush upon a leem's nest, horter Khardun! You are a hyrpaktun. Keep close. I may have great use for a kampeon such as yourself, and Nath the Dorvenhork."

Seg had not offered to hire out as a mercenary.

By rescuing them and landing them safely in civilization, Obolya the Zorcanim had discharged the duty laid on him by the Laws of the River. He had contracted to take Milsi on to Mewsansmot; nobody else. If Seg accompanied Milsi, he'd have to pay his passage, always assuming Obolya cared to find room for him.

As for the rest of them, they would have to fend for themselves. They were penniless, with the scraps of clothing found for them from Obolya's wardrobe chests, without occupations. They could easily be taken up again as slaves—vagrants, no-goods, people without visible means of support. This Kov Llipton sounded like your stiff and upright guardian of the laws, such as many Kovs when assuming the regency became in a twinkling.

Cautiously, Seg inspected the condition of his purse. The gold he'd taken from the Coup Blag had been in his estimate enough to last him a long time, given that copper and silver were the more common metals of currency. He could hand out three gold pieces per person, and leave himself with ten. H'm. . . . Once you'd been a noble yourself you tended to forget about a lot of the more unpleasant aspects of money, as he'd explained to the two dinkus.

He still would not think too hard of what Milsi had told him of her child. Well, of course she had a child! Didn't that make sense? She was a married woman. Of course she was. She had said that her husband was dead; she did not specify how or the circumstances.

Seg didn't want to know. Nothing had changed in his estimation. He still determined to carry on with what he had sworn.

The mercenaries hired by Obolya congregated in a group under the staring eyeless heads on their stakes. They wrangled with one another, and their talk was hard and bitter. Most were local lads, trying to get into the mercenary trade; there was just the one paktun with the silver mortil-head at his throat. He had assumed command.

The burden of their complaints could be summed up by: "Since King Crox cleaned up the river there is little employment for us. It is hard to find work for an honest mercenary."

The paktun, Norolger the Arm, said: "Since the great wars finished all paktuns have seen lean times. There must be work for us up in the plains. I heard from my twin recently who is in North Pandahem. He said there was plenty of work there, although he did not or could not say whose army was recruiting."

"Then let us go there! You will lead us, Norolger the Arm, and be our Deldar!"

"And who will pay our passage?"

The Chulik Nath the Dorvenhork interrupted to say: "If you wish to sail around Pandahem to the north, you will sail render-infested seas. You will find ready hire among the masters of the merchant ships, or even in the swordships if you are very skilled."

Two of the mercenaries, little more than coys, said they were going home, and although they gave the reason as a longing to taste once more the delights of their mothers' cooking, Seg, for one, suspected other motives. Being a paktun on Kregen, an honest profession, was not an easy life to lead.

The other mercenaries wandered off still wrangling about what best to do.

Seg looked hard at Khardun. The Khibil would be the toughest. Once he had accepted, the others would follow. Khardun the Franch, as his cognomen suggested, was a very bright spark indeed who thought a great deal of himself.

"Khardun! What is your hire fee these days?"

Khardun had no need to explain that while Chuliks might be trained up from birth to be exemplary fighting men, any Khibil was worth at least as much, if not more. By reason of his smartness, of course . . . This was not a generally held opinion. Chuliks and Pachaks looked to be paid at least a third more than a Khibil. This general opinion was stated, with a firmness that held severe protocol in the address, by the Dorvenhork.

Seg kept the exasperation out of his face and voice. He'd thought he'd handled this giving of gold to the dratted Khibil cleverly, and instead had raised a howling argument.

"When mercenaries are hiring on in times of short supply," Khardun snapped out, intemperately, "many cherished opinions are shattered."

"Here there is an oversupply of mercenaries."

Seg butted in. "Dratted good pay for a mercenary is a silver piece a day. You'd get a lot less here. A Chulik can look, as Nath well knows, for twelve a week. A Khibil will take nine."

"And an apim will take seven!" flared Khardun.

"Oh," said Seg. "I'd stand out for eight."

The Rapa, Rafikhan, fluffed up his feathers and said morosely: "We Rapas are paid the standard one silver piece a day, six a week. I have been paid nine, once, when I went for a varterman and—well, never mind that."

During this conversation Diomb stood, first on one leg, then on the other, listening avidly. He had slung his blowpipe over his back, broken down into four pieces.

"Listen to me," said Seg, and at his tone they all swiveled to regard him, silently. "I intend to give three gold pieces to each of the party with us. That will help them on their way home." He glared at the fighting men in the party, well-knowing that the rest would accept his offer gladly and with thanks. "As for you paktuns. I need to hire on a bodyguard. I shall pay you each three gold pieces. I leave it a paktun's honor for each of you to decide just how long you will serve for that amount. Is that understood? Then *Queyd-arn-tung!*"*

---

* Queyd-arn-tung! No more need be said.

They goggled at him for a bit, surprised—yet the Chulik, remembering their first meeting and the ominous steadiness of Seg's bow on him in the boat, gave a salute with due punctilio.

"So be it, by Likshu the Treacherous."

"By Horato the Potent! So be it!"

"By Rhapaporgolam the Reiver of Souls! So be it!"

Seg nodded, brusquely.

The others in the party crowded round, jabbering away, excited, filling the air with clamor, all thanking horter Seg for his munificence. Seg felt around for his belt pouch and the purse within. The latch was already undone and he hauled out the purse, heavy with gold.

Umtig stepped a little forward, the eight-armed spinlikl, Lord Clinglin, draped around his neck and shoulders. The Och smirked pridefully.

"I thank you most sincerely for your most generous gesture in presenting me with three gold pieces, horter Seg. I shall, of course, repay you." He laughed that high, almost giggling Och laugh. "Oh, and horter Seg, you have already paid me." In his supple fingers three gold croxes glowed.

"What!" Seg looked into his purse, looked at the Och, saw the gold—and he laughed. He laughed with his head thrown back and his huge chest expanded, his shock of black hair dancing.

"You hulu!"

"Aye!"

Khardun looked down his foxy nose at the Och.

"And if you were a mercenary, Umtig, you would receive a mere three or four silver pieces a week."

"Four or five!" spluttered Umtig, cackling with his own ingenuity at his trade. Seg hadn't felt a thing.

Now Diomb stepped forward, bright and expectant.

Seg sighed.

"I do not know, good Diomb, I really do not know."

"But, Seg, I wish to earn my hire. If I need money so that Bamba and I may eat, well, then—"

"You will not go short while I still have gold."

"That is not the same thing, as I now understand."

The Khibil laughed. "A copper ob a day, doms?"

The Chulik polished up his tusk with his thumb.

"Mayhap. It is no concern of mine."

"Now," said Seg, lifting his voice, "as we all have gold in our pockets let us go out and put some wine and meat into our bellies."

"Aye!"

He felt disappointment when Milsi indicated that she and Malindi would be staying within the accommodation offered in the wharf area for paying guests. She offered no explanation apart from a disinclination to venture into the city away from Obolya's boat. He caught the impression that she imagined the rapscallion section of the party with Seg would riot all their money away in a low-class tavern and be thrown out, arrested for drunken and disorderly, or in some way offend the laws. The shadow of Kov Llipton hovered unseen over them.

Many of the main streets possessed wooden sidewalks raised on stilts, and some had decorative arcades and papishin-leaved roofs. When the rains came, it appeared, the good folk of Nalvinlad took care of themselves.

As his comrades started off out of the wharf area, some of them danced little jigs upon the boardwalk. Seg stared after them and turned back to Milsi. "Truly is it said by San Blarnoi, my lady, that a human person is like an onion, layer of secrets wrapped within layer. I shall, of course, not accompany those rogues—"

"Oh, do not be silly, Seg! Go if you want to."

Diomb looked back, waving farewell to Bamba, for the first time since they had left their homes in the forest. Bamba stood with Malindi. Milsi looked cross.

"I do not want you saying that I kept you from all your enjoyments."

" It will not be much of an enjoyment if you are not there to share it."

"A noisy tavern, no doubt a foul dopa den, dancing girls, caff, all manner of spectacles put on called entertainment?"

"I am not in the habit of frequenting dopa dens. Dopa is a liquor so fiery as to make anyone a fighting fool, and, I think you imagine I am enough of that already—my lady."

The movement of her chin would have, in a less composed woman, been a toss of the head. She bit her lip and looked away.

"Go, Seg. Your friends will leave without you."

"They are all our friends, surely?"

"After you have paid them gold—most surely!"

"I only did—"

"Quite! Now Malindi and I are off to the little clothing arcade just over there, where we will outfit ourselves, and Bamba, too. Remberee, Seg."

And she turned with Malindi and Bamba following and walked off with that superb lithe swing of her hips.

Seg did not swear aloud. But, to himself, using one of the Bogandur's favorites, he said: "By the disgusting diseased liver and lights of Makki Grodno! —What a woman!"

# CHAPTER TEN

## Concerning an ob and a toc

The Rokveil's Ank was not quite as bad as Milsi had predicted the tavern would be; not quite.

It was situated on a side turning from the Street of Anchor Stones, where the sidewalks were fallen away here and there. When the rains came the roadway became a quagmire so tenacious that even a Quoffa, hauling with might and main, would never shift his cart harnessed to him by chains. The papishin leaf roof resounded to the uproar. Inside the tavern the wooden walls seeped water. No one appeared to care.

No dopa was served here.

Seg would not have entered had dopa been served, not because he was too prudish ever to enter a dopa den but because the almost inevitable fights tended to a sad and messy conclusion. Dopa dens, as he had come to know could yield secrets and offer fine plucked rascals to be used as unwitting tools in intrigues.

The tables were scrubbed clean, the pots and

jugs of a similar cleanly style, and the various brews far superior to anything so far encounted along the Kazzchun River. This was only a small unpretentious tavern a stone's throw from the waterfront; but this was the capital city.

A Sylvie came in swirling gauzes and clanging bangles and danced erotically, and a performing animal with heavy chains was prodded by red-hot irons into dancing, and a troupe of jugglers threw balls and hoops and firebrands about and. . . . Seg sat slumped into the corner of a settle and moped about the words he'd had with Milsi.

In all the uproar among the fumes of wine and ale and the blue smells of cooking from the kitchen, the hot fat sizzling in pans as food was hurried by serving wenches to the tables, Seg gradually found himself listening to the different conversations going on.

Naturally, one of the main topics was the capture and summary execution of the renders. Kov Llipton had acted very smartly there, the news flying up and down the river in no time. But, it was clear, even amid all this bustle and the titillation of fresh gossip, everyone's mind dwelt upon the absence of the king and queen. The river was not the same without the guiding hand of King Crox, no matter how smartly the regent, Kov Llipton, acted.

No one knew much about conditions in the Snarly Hills, and a variety of opinions were expressed. That the place was infested with bandits was certain sure, and the king had stopped that, may the good Pandrite be praised. But how drikingers within their forest fastnesses could interfere with river traffic remained a puzzle, and the few land routes

were hazardous enough at the best of times. Seg
sat, drinking carefully, and he noticed that for all
their big talk, Khardun, Rafikhan and the Dorvenhork also drank sparingly. They did, however, eat
hugely.

Seg felt it would be less than politic—at the
very least!—to mention that a Witch of Loh sat
like an evil spider at the center of the Snarly Hills
in the Coup Blag.

Nath the Dorvenhork caught the attention of a
serving wench and asked if The Rokveil's Ank
served huliper pie.

"No, master. Squish pie, celene flan, jooshas—"
She would have rattled out the menu, but the
Dorvenhork nodded in his dour Chulik way and
said, "Squish."

" Huliper Pie," said Rafikhan, leaning forward.
"You have been in the army, horter Nath."

"It is no secret. A Chulik follows the guiding
hand of Shum of the Four Tusks into whatever
fortune brings."

Diomb was agog to taste all the varied delights
of civilized cooking.

"Squish pie," said Seg. "I have a comrade, a
very great comrade, who dotes on squish pie. Yet
his taboos deny him the pleasure without penance,
so that he spends bur after bur standing on his
head."

Diomb laughed delightedly. He had proved an
object of interest to the denizens of the tavern for
only a short time. Most of them had seen dinkus
before, captured and brought in as curiosities. Times
changed, and no doubt the little people of the
forest would soon be setting up in business in
Nalvinlad. If good King Crox were here, now. . . .

When Seg's roast ponsho and momolams ar-rived at the table he looked at the platter, frowning.

"What is it, Seg?" demanded Diomb.

"A strange fashion this, to be sure."

Diomb summoned the serving wench by the simple expedient of showing her a copper ob be-tween his nimble fingers. He was learning the ways of civilization. The girl, she was apim with smudgy cheeks, ample bosom, stringy hair, dressed in a simple gray tunic, and she could carry a tray with ten jugs of ale one-handed, came over at once.

"What is this food?" demanded Diomb.

"It is Weeping Ponsho, master."

Seg said: "How is the dish cooked?"

"Why, master, I know that, although I am but a serving girl. You slash the ponsho and stuff the cuts with herbs. You cut the momolams into slices and then you roast the meat above the vegetables on a rack so that all the fats and goodness drip down." She looked proud in her own knowledge.

"No doubt, one day, you will be the cook here." Seg stirred the mess with his knife. "I will eat this. But I prefer ponsho roast whole, or quar-tered respectably, with the momolams halved length-ways and arranged around the meat."

"I have heard of that, master. We think it—" Then she stopped, clearly frightened at her willful-ness in what she was about to say. You did not contradict a patron. The landlord had a hard and heavy switch hanging at the back of the kitchen door.

All this time she had not taken her eyes off the ob in Diomb's fingers, going flickety-flick up and down in the way he'd copied, the coin a dazzle.

He flicked it to her and, with the unerring aim of a forest marksman he shied it into the cleavage of her gray tunic. She wiggled, laughed in an affected way, and said, "Thank you, master, may the good Pandrite reward you."

Khardun the Franch looked at Diomb, and Seg, watching, saw that the Khibil smiled a genuine smile, albeit a foxy one.

"You want to be more careful with your money, young Diomb. Not all gold comes as easily as that from horter Seg."

"Oh?"

"Why, yes. Didn't you see the look on that girl's face? She never gets more than a toc as a tip, and you get six tocs for one copper ob."

Diomb shoved his blowpipe up his shoulder out of the way, and leaned back against the settle. "I thank you, horter Khardun, for your information. A toc is one of these, then?" And he held up the tiny coin to inspect it more closely.

Somewhat morosely, Seg struck into his meal. A Fristle fifi came in to sing a song and the taproom more or less quieted down to listen. In her melodious meowling way she sang through: "The Lay of Faerly the Ponsho Farmer's Daughter." Then she warbled, "Black is White and White is Black," concerning the doings of the miller's and the sweep's wives. She finished up with a little ditty about a girl who so loved a boy on the opposite bank of the Kazzchun River that she essayed to swim and risk the perils of the jaws in the water. Her courage and love so impressed the goddess Pavishkeemi that she came down from her house in Panachreem, the home of the deities of Pandahem, and spread her shush-chiff across the

waters. This elegant flowing garment provided a
safe way for the love-sick girl, whose name, in the
fashion of Kregen, changed from region to region.

This song was known as "The Shush-chiff of
Pavishkeemi the Beloved."

The Fristle fifi sang well and the applause that
followed was genuine. Coins showered about her
feet. The Fristle with the party, Naghan the Slippy,
was so carried away he joyfully threw the fifi a
whole shining silver Dhem. Diomb did not notice
this. Mindful of Khardun's words, he threw over
the little copper toc.

The girl saw. She bent down with a single
graceful motion, picked the toc from the floor, and
with a scornful gesture, flung it back at Diomb.

"What—?" exclaimed the dinko, bemused.

Khardun blew out his reddish whiskers. "There
are degrees of recompense within the world, young
Diomb, and you have just demonstrated two of
them—in the wrong order."

"I suppose I will understand this silly world,
one day?"

The young mercenaries who had served as boat
guards for the short trip upriver now came in.
They looked disgusted. Deeming the rest of his
river journey safe, Obolya had paid them off.
They had money which they proceeded to squander.

"Onkers," said Khardun. "They will learn."

The paktun, Norolger the Arm, whom they had
elected as their Deldar to command them, made a
half-hearted attempt to restrain the lavish spending.
But his heart was not in it.

"By the Blade of Kurin!" he said, wiping the
froth from his mouth. "Life is hard, doms, exceed-
ing hard."

A man wearing a coat of sewn skins sitting just along the wall hitched his cudgel forward and lifted his jug.

"If you seek work, paktuns, the wolves are out along the plains up past Mewsansmot."

The paktuns swiveled to stare at this unwelcome intrusion upon their conspicuous misery.

"Wolves?" said Norolger. "We are paktuns, not animal catchers."

The wolves they were talking about, Seg decided, must really be werstings, and they were ferocious and vicious and yet could be tamed by man into hunting packs. Runaway criminals and fugitives of all kinds trembled when they heard the yeowling of the wersting pack upon their heels.

He scraped the platter clean and pushed it aside. Before he reached for the looshas pudding he took a swingeing draught of ale. It was probably correct for Milsi not to have accompanied him. But, then, had she done so he would have walked farther on and sought out a more respectable inn. He thought of Milsi, and found he was looking forward to meeting her daughter. For quite clearly her daughter was the real reason Milsi was so determined to go up to Mewsansmot where the werstings prowled.

Milsi, with her new handmaid Malindi and the charming dinka Bamba, found satisfaction at the warm welcome accorded them in the clothing arcade. The proprietor, a Lamnia called Orlan Felminyer, brushed up his pale yellow fur and smiled and spread his wares. His wife, Alenci, took the three into a back room where they could strip off their old clothes, thankfully, and then with many wriggles and sighs, and exclamations of delight, try on brand new clothes.

Bamba was determined not to wear her bark apron again. She declared that if she was to be a woman of the world then she must dress accordingly.

Milsi's gold procured first-class service and sumptuous apparel. In the end, they bought a chestful.

"Have it taken down to horter Obolya's boat, please, horter Felminyer."

"It shall be done, my lady."

The twin suns threw their twin shadows across the boardwalk as they emerged. The rains had broomed away and the sky was clearing. Out in the alley between arcade and wharfside a file of soldiers marched up, halted at a sharp word of command, grounded their spears.

Milsi realized that Kov Llipton did, indeed, run the kingdom tightly. An officer—he was a Hikdar—walked up the few steps onto the boardwalk. He was apim, ruddy-featured, thrusting, wearing half-armor and carrying an arsenal of weapons in the Kregan way. He touched a forefinger to the peak of his helmet and spoke to Milsi.

"My lady. You are from Obolya Metromin's boat?"

"That is correct, Mikdar."

His ruddy features darkened. "My apologies, my lady. Llahal. I am Hikdar Northag ti Hovensmot. I seek information from you concerning your traveling companions."

"Llahal Hikdar Northag. How may I assist you?"

She looked at him quite calmly. He wore an ornate plume of brown and white feathers in his helmet, and although they were not arbora feathers, they looked splendid. Even the swods in the ranks, the ordinary footsoldiers, wore a piling bunch of brown and white feathers in their bronze helmets.

"I have just asked you. Where are the people from Obolya's boat?"

"Gone drinking in some tavern or other."

His gaze bore down on her. At that moment Milsi felt cold. He did not look quite the same fine upright soldierly person her first impression had conveyed.

"Very well."

He swung away, bellowed unpleasantly at the Deldar at the head of the file—it was an audo of ten men—and jumped off the boardwalk. Milsi watched them until the last clump of brown and white feathers vanished past the end of a warehouse with a broken crane over the upper doors.

"What could that have been all about, my lady?" ventured Malindi in her simple way.

"I do not know," snapped Milsi, crossly.

Bamba smoothed down her new green dress with the orange bows and the yellow lace. Milsi had been quite unable to part the dinka from the abomination.

"I did not like them at all," said Bamba, with a spurt of fierceness. "Men like that have chased us in the forest."

"Yes, and I daresay men like your Diomb have shot poisoned darts at them!"

"Milsi!"

"Oh, yes, very well. I didn't mean to be so sharp. But I am worried. What, in the name of the foul Armipand, did they really want?"

The three women began slowly to walk back to the wharfside where Obolya's boat was tied up. The smells of the river grew stronger, mingling with the brisk smells of the wharf, of which fish was the most prominent.

Milsi stopped so suddenly Malindi crashed into her.

"I am sorry, my lady—"

"Enough of that, Malindi! Of course! What a fool I am!"

"What is it?" cried Bamba.

"It has to be so. That rast of a villain Ortyg the Undlefar. They must have questioned him. He told them—oh, I can see it all!"

Bamba looked nervously unhappy; Malindi started to cry.

"We must warn Seg and the others!" said Milsi, and she straight away started to run swiftly along the alley. Gripping her skirts high, head up, she ran panting with passionate fury toward the city.

# CHAPTER ELEVEN

## Knives

"We are a bedraggled-looking bunch," observed Seg, feeling the food inside him and the ale cheerful in his blood. "Let us go along to the souks and buy ourselves some decent clothes."

"Aye," rumbled the Dorvenhork. "Clothes are all very well. But there is a greater need we lack."

He had no need to place his broad yellow hand upon the fire-sharpened wooden stake at his side. In almost any location on Kregen a man needed a weapon, preferably a small arsenal of weapons. Kregans habitually carry enough weapons for the task ahead, not less, not more. If a blade breaks in your hands, and you have no other weapons to draw. . . . Equally, no Kregan will willingly burden himself with junk he does not need.

"Agreed," said Khardun.

They rose from the table, pushing the heavy wooden thing away with no difficulty. They stood up, stretching their legs. Only the Chulik belched.

"Weapons first," he said, and there was no argument, not even from Seg.

"All the same," pointed out Khardun. "We will be able to afford precious little."

"A knife, maybe that is all we will need for a beginning. These wooden spears will serve, I judge. As for an axe—"

"Well," observed Rafikhan, blowing out his feathers. "We will never afford a single sword between us."

"You will pardon me, doms," said Umtig. He stroked the spinlikl upon his breast. "I will return to the boat. I had an eye to Master Orlan Felminyer's arcade."

They watched him trot off without comment, merely calling the polite remberees.

Among the many different folk from all up and down the Kazzchun River they excited no particular interest. There were half-naked men and women seeking to earn their daily food, folk who slept under the piles of the sidewalks, folk who were as adept at stealing the copper ob as at carrying the burden from the wharfside.

Very very few men walked about without a weapon of some kind, even though very many of the poorer folk carried merely a heavy bludgeon.

The roadways steamed. The radiance of the suns beat down and very soon the gluey mud would return to its hard-baked consistency. Up ahead the walkways led into that part of the city where the souks and covered alleys ran in a confusing tangle. These areas of cities, known as the aracloins, harbored commerce, money and villainy.

These particular aracloins in Nalvinlad were not extensive and it was abundantly clear that Kov

Llipton kept a close eye on them. Parties of soldiers wearing blue and white feathers in their helmets could be seen here and there ready to squelch
the first incipient riot.

The party with Seg walked along very meekly
when they passed the soldiers. Old-hand paktuns
knew when to make themselves small. Particularly
when they carried no weapons in their fists.

The odd thing was that while most of the party
of ordinary folk whom Seg had rescued did not go
first to the souks of weaponry, instead trotting off
to find new clothes, the Relt, mild and gentle,
Caphlander the Quill, went with the paktuns.

As he said, "While I am with you, whom I
venture to call comrades, I feel safe. And I must
buy a penknife."

They guffawed, and jollied him along. But they
all sensed the innate wholesomeness of Caphlander,
with his innocent beaked face and the yellow feathers rounding his eyes into bright intelligence.

"This looks likely," said Khardun, halting
precipitately. They all looked at the entrance to the
store, one of many lining the sides of the souk.
The sign said that one Jezbellandur the Iarvin provided the best weapons in all Croxdrin. Seg noticed that the word Croxdrin in the ornately
embellished hyr-Kregish, was recently painted and
already some of the base paint was flaking away to
reveal dimmer lettering beneath. That would be
the word Nalvindrin, without a doubt.

An audo—only eight of them—of soldiers
marched past with careful looks at Seg and his
people. These soldiers wore green and yellow
feathers. Farther on, chasing a couple of idiots

caught thieving, a group of soldiers wearing green and white feathers rushed on, hullabalooing.

Everyone stood back as the rout passed.

"How is it, horter Hundle," Seg said to the boat-master, "that there are differently colored feathers?"

"Oh, each great lord of the land recruits his own forces and allocates a certain number under Kov Llipton to the proper policing of the city. The blue and whites, they are Kov Llipton's men."

"I see."

They all trooped into Master Jezbellandur's bazaar, and gawped around at the splendid display of weaponry upon the walls and in open-fronted cases about the wooden floor.

Master Jezbellandur himself, nick-named the Iarvin, came forward rubbing his hands together. He clearly was a man of substance, a man who knew himself to be smart, clever, supreme master of his trade, and, at the same time, he managed to express a devoted attention to the wants of his clients.

He summed up this sorry band in no time at all. "Not a pair of copper obs to rub together between them," he said to himself. But he bowed. If they did have a pair of copper obs, he'd have them off them, that he promised.

Khardun, like the other paktuns, had patronized places like this many times before. He was brisk.

"We need first quality knives, horter. And we would like to test them in your salle."

"Knives. Well, I have the finest selection—"

"Good. That is settled. Lead on."

So it was that they were ushered into the salle, a large, square, bare room at the rear of the premises.

The floor, although gleamingly clean, was not polished. Sand stood ready in buckets to be strewn. No one else at the moment was in the place. Khardun nodded at the targets, stuffed with grasses.

"Knives that cut, stab, and throw."

"At once, horters."

The cases were produced by a bent-backed Och who contrived to balance two cases at a time. The knives were duly inspected and then test-hurled at the targets.

Seg wandered across to a corner and sat on a chair. Business must be poor for the weapons-trader to concede so much time to men merely buying knives. The racks of swords and axes and spears, of armor and helmets, remained unopened.

The door crashed open and a madwoman rushed in, shrieking.

"The guards are coming! We must run, hide—quick, oh, quick!"

Seg leaped up. He stared. The woman wore a brand new dress hiked up to her knees, mud-splashed and stained. He choked.

"Milsi!"

"They think we are pirates! The guards are coming!"

Umtig the Lock, clasping his spinlikl, sidled in after Milsi. That, then explained how she had found them. The little Och thief would follow their trail with no trouble. Malindi and Bamba ran in, crying, and Diomb rushed across to them.

"Hurry!" Milsi called, agonized, and whirled, her eyes enormous, her hands leaving the hem of her dress and going in horror to her mouth.

The guards clumped in, hard, spears leveled, the brown and white feathers in their helmets low-

ering as they bent ready to thrust. Milsi exclaimed
in despair that her attempt to warn Seg had proved
futile. Seg put a brown hand up to his bow.

"Do not attempt to resist, rast!" The Hikdar,
brave in his armor, stepped forward. Milsi could
see that he had reinforced his original audo, and
now a rank of bowmen bent their bows upon Seg
and his comrades. "You are charged with being
renders. Your heads will adorn the stakes at the
city walls!"

Seg took his hand away. He stepped forward.

"There is a mistake, Hikdar. We are peaceable
men, stranded in the river. We are not pirates—"

"Shastum! Silence, you yetch."

"But we can explain it all!"

The bowmen were commanded by a second
Hikdar, corpulent, sweating in his armor, his brown
and white feathers far grander than the first Hikdar's.
He stepped up to the side of the first Hikdar and
whispered in his ear.

Seg just stood, poised, alert, watching. He and
the comrades with him were at a clear disadvantage.
They had no real weapons. These soldiers, despite
the finery, were well-armed. He noticed that the
bowmen had spurs fixed to their tall brown boots.
This puzzled him. How would cavalry be employed along the river to make the expense of the
arm worthwhile? Rafikhan had mentioned that there
were swarths available for riders farther north.
These were the so-called two-legged swarths of
Pandahem. The true swarth had four legs, a
powerful, humped reptilian saddle animal with a
heavy wedge-shaped head. The Pandahem two-
legged variety possessed four limbs, of course; the
forelimbs were nowhere as well developed as the

afterlimbs, giving the swarths a faint resemblance to sleeths.

These silly fragile thoughts flowed through his head as he watched what went on.

The porcine Hikdar laughed. Seg did not care for that laugh.

"Well, Northag? What do you say?"

"I—you're confident nothing would come out, Pafnut?"

"Of course not. A bit of fun. Then, afterwards, well—who's going to ask questions? Trylon Muryan?"

"The Trylon? He wouldn't care—no, you're right." This unpleasant Hikdar Northag licked his lips. Then: "My swods. I'm not sure about them—"

"It's my lads who'll be into it, never fear. Send yours out into the bazaar." Sweat showed in the wrinkles on Hikdar Pafnut's fat cheeks.

Seg braced himself. He detested the so-called soldiers who harassed the weak folk of the world. Vicious cowards like that gave soldiers a bad name. The kind of soldier Seg understood was devoted to protecting others from those who would kill or enslave or rob. It was quite clear this unhealthy bunch were going to have some fun with their victims in the salle. Leeming, they called it, a rough, nasty knock-about that could turn ugly.

Khardun knew. He said, "I judge this Northag offal to be lily-livered, and easily led by this thing called Pafnut." He spoke so that the soldiers could not hear him. "Brace yourselves, fanshos, brassud!"

"Aye," growled the Dorvenhork. "I mark me this Pafnut and will deliver his tripes to Likshu the Treacherous, personally."

Hikdar Northag rapped out a command and his

Deldar, poker-faced, marched out the spearmen. The leveled bows of Pafnut's command remained spanned on the party at the other side of the salle. Seg put an arm around Milsi. The gesture was completely unaffected.

"The men over here!" shouted Pafnut. He looked bloated. "Bratch!"

Obediently, the men bratched. They walked smartly across the unpolished floor, covered all the way by the bent bows and the steel-tipped arrows, expecting to feel fists, or boots, or the flats of swords beating on them as the swods had their fun.

"Outside!" Pafnut's thick lips glistened, foam flew.

Instantly, Seg and the others saw what was afoot.

Only Diomb failed to grasp what was intended.

Now the Dorvenhork was an archer. He was as well aware as Seg of the menace of those drawn bows.

"Outside!" shrieked Pafnut. His Deldar lowered his bow, let the arrow slide down the shaft to grip it left-handed, and drew his sword with his right hand. He moved up to take command of the party.

He picked on Seg. Over the noise of heavy breathing, the chink of metal, the sudden uproar, Seg heard Milsi's voice from the far side of the salle. "Oh, Seg!"

Seg yelled. "Knives!"

He kicked the Deldar in the guts, swiveled, smashed the nearest bowman across the bridge of his nose, feeling the string smart. His own knife whipped up in a blur of speed and flew to stand out full in Pafnut's porcine face.

Other knives flew. In the instant between Seg's call and the hurling of the knives, the soldiers had failed to respond. When they did loose, they were dead men loosing at shadows.

Milsi and Bamba ran across instantly, and Malindi followed. The men were already hard at work snatching up bows, swords, quivers of arrows.

"We came here to buy weapons," exulted Khardun. "And these onkers gave us theirs free!"

Milsi said, a hard note in her voice: "Does anyone claim this dead Pafnut's rapier and main gauche?"

No one appeared to know much of the outlandish weapons. Seg said: "They are yours, my lady. But I would that you do not go too froward when we blatter those outside."

"Our best plan, Seg the Horkandur, will be to leave this evil place by the back door."

Seg looked around. He saw the lads of his party plundering what each required of armor and weapons. He saw the dead men. He saw the way Diomb and Bamba still had not understood what was intended. "Evil place? No, my lady. Not the place, the kleeshes who came in for sport."

"You are right, quibble though you must at a time like this! Come on! Let us escape."

"The lady Milsi is right," said Khardun. "They will think, those with the squeamish stomachs outside in the bazaar, that we are being beaten in a little leeming. Let us go now, and take our revenge later."

And Seg laughed.

"Revenge, good Khardun! Look around you!"

"Oh, aye, well, by Horato the Potent! I shall not forget these rasts who wear brown and white."

"Nor I!" said the Chulik with great menace.

"Are we all ready, then, fanshos?"

"Aye, ready."

Seg cast a gloomy eye on the bows still lying upon the floor. They were dorven bows, compound reflex, good enough for a first class archer. Their arrows were too short for his own Lohvian longbow. Still, he was running short of shafts. Philosophically, he retrieved a bow that looked as though it had been cared for, and with it two quivers of arrows. These he slung on his back, then turned and faced his comrades.

"Wenda! Let's go!"

When they had all vanished out of the rear door, along that clean and unpolished floor lay a scattering trail of ripped off brown and white feathers.

# CHAPTER TWELVE

## The Law of the River

It is said over much of Kregen and widely believed that Chuliks have no sense of humanity. Trained from birth as they are to the military art, they possess a strict sense of order, of the need for rules and regulations, for the necessity of ladders of command to avoid confusion. Their codes of conduct are different from those of many other races. They have nothing of the fanatical dedication to honor, to their nikobi, of the Pachaks. They have nothing to do with the races who change colors upon the battlefield as the swing and sway of conflict brings victory or defeat.

Over the seasons Seg had been nurturing a growing conviction that the Chuliks were misjudged. Their own harsh upbringing and sense of values denied them the outgoing frankness that might have changed general opinion. They could not readily accept a proffered hand of friendship.

When Nath Chandarl the Dorvenhork said, ''I would not have witnessed the outrage to the little

dinko, Bamba,'' Seg could see what the Chulik
meant. He was not, in these later seasons of greater
wisdom, surprised as he would have been even a
few short seasons ago.

For the Rapa, Rafikhan, a different set of mores
had to be applied. Given the license, it was common knowledge what would happen to a woman of
another race if she was thrown into the Rapa court.
But Rafikhan had joined in the fight with relish,
his flung knife extinguishing a brown and white
feathered soldier, his ferocious hands and beak
destroying another.

As for the Khibil, Khardun the Franch, his innate sense of superiority had motivated him to
protect his friends. Amnesty for wrongdoers was
very foreign to a Khibil's philosophy.

The Fristle, Naghan the Slippy, although not a
mercenary, had played his part. He said he was a
metalworker, and detested the river, and Seg believed him, willy-nilly.

Now they sailed up the Kazzchun River in
Obolya's boat, paying their way in solid silver
Dhems, and kept a watchful lookout for pursuit.
The brown and white feathered soldiery of Trylon
Muryan would be after them if no other lord felt
inclined to send his paktuns in pursuit.

Obolya the Zorcanim, of course, remained in
total ignorance of the malefactions of the ne'er-do-
wells who took passage in his boat. He labored
under the impression that he had hired on the
Chulik and the Khibil. No one disabused him of
the notion.

As Seg said, ''I give you thanks, friends, for
your courage and help. You earned your hire, to
speak in base commercial paktunish terms, exceed-

ingly well. But, for now, why not take a holiday from my service and serve Obolya?"

This could be done in honor and so was done.

That it might have unforeseen consequences did not escape Seg, but he felt it to be the best way of making sure of Obolya's friendship.

A mercenary does not leave a dead body lying around abandoned when time and circumstance give him the opportunity to make sure the poor dead fellow has no more assistance to offer.

Seg insisted that the money taken from the dead soldiers should be shared equally.

Khardun laughed. "That is as it should be. Then we are all equally implicated."

The Relt, Caphlander, quivered at this. But he said: "I cannot strike a blow. But, doms, I stand implicated and although I want none of the cash, I am your comrade still."

They made him take his share.

This little band were fugitives from the law as administered by Kov Llipton. Seg expressed himself as mightily dissatisfied with the famous Law of the River.

Milsi corrected him.

"The Law of the River is unwritten. It is a common bond between all who sail the brown waters. We help one another. But the law of the land, as given by King Crox and now administered by Kov Llipton, is another matter. In that, I think you err also, my Horkandur."

"Oh? How so?"

"Those evil men were from the retinue of Trylon Muryan. He hates the Kov, as the Kov hates the Trylon." Then she passed a hand across her forehead. "I wish I knew if Llipton could be trusted."

"You said you had no reason to distrust him. And, anyway, Milsi—by the Veiled Froyvil!—you are the queen's lady in waiting. Surely you should tell this Kov what has happened to the king and queen?"

"And then?"

"H'm. I see."

In this part of Paz on this side of Kregen the highest noble rank was a High Kov. Then came a Kov followed by a Vad. After that rank came a Trylon and then a Strom. There were three more ranks in the higher nobility, Rango, Elten and Amak. As for the lesser nobility, that varied widely, names and positions changing, it seemed, with every individual country.

Seg had had his fill of nobility. He'd willingly forsaken his overlordship on the question of slavery, and his good comrade, Turko the Shield, had taken over and was no doubt bringing a harsher hand to bear on forcing the dissidents into line with imperial policy.

There was no doubt about it. Even though he joyed in the company of Milsi and made the most of every moment of this journey, he sorely missed the companionship of his comrades. Inch, whose taboos made him do extraordinary things, Turko the Shield, Korero the Shield, Oby, Balass the Hawk, Naghan the Gnat, young tearaway Vomanus of Vindelka, all his blade comrades, and, of course, most of all his old dom, the Bogandur himself.

Well, he'd see Milsi safely home, and then find out what the fates held for him. He noticed that the nearer they sailed to Mewsansmot the more edgy and nervous she became.

He was well aware that he had been indulging himself in this knight-errantry. Unsure though he might be about what would happen, he was sufficiently aware of himself and his wants to know that he needed Milsi. There was no use disguising that. Since he had lost Thelda, grieving for her on her long last journey to the Ice Floes of Sicce, he had grown emotionally callous. He'd taken a sneaking amusement from the speculations of acquaintances that he might marry Jilian Sweet-Tooth. That had never been in his plan of life.

No. No, he could find happiness with Milsi. Yet the secret she clearly harbored troubled him. Was it merely the existence of her daughter? That had no possible influence on him; he would love to meet Milsi's daughter, be a new father to her, bring her into the family of Drayseg, and Valin and Silda. And, by the same token, no doubt he and they would be engulfed in the relations Milsi must have somewhere in Kregen.

Just as they reached the last stretch before Mewsansmot, Milsi found Seg right forrard in the bows where the gangplank lay stowed. He watched the brown water and the ripples, spotting the swift slither of great bodies below the surface, the gape of fangs. The capital of Croxdrin, Nalvinlad, was built where the forest ended and the plains began. The schinkitree paddled now between the banks, low and bushy, and beyond them extended the plains out to the distant horizons.

"Seg. We shall soon be home."

"Home? Your home, Milsi, not mine."

"And not mine, really, either. You must have guessed I wish to see my daughter, Mishti. You are a parent; you understand how our heart trembles for our children."

"I do."

"I left her with friends—Clawsangs—and yet I worry and worry—"

"Do not fret so, Milsi. Clawsangs are bonny fighters. We had a group with us in the Coup Blag. Skort the Clawsang and his people. They were trapped behind a falling stone. I trust they escaped as did we, for the Bogandur mentioned them as being in the jungle."

"So do I!"

The brown water slid by and the twin suns, Zim and Genodras, poured down their mingled streaming lights. Seg drew a breath.

"When you have assured yourself that your daughter, the lady Mishti, is safe, then what will you do?"

"I do not know!"

"Ah! Then—" Seg swallowed. He started again, and again trailed off. He wet his lips. Then, remembering he was supposed to be a bold brave paktun wandering Bowman warrior, he said: "My lady Milsi. I think you know of my affection for you. Well, that affection is grown—"

"No, Seg! No! Stop."

"But—"

"Do not say anything. I cannot answer. I cannot!"

He felt the granite falling onto his heart.

"Perhaps you love another?"

"Oh, you fool, Seg Segutorio! Cheap words from a cheap farce out of the theater souk!"

"Maybe. I thought you could—"

"I could, I could . . . But it is—no, Seg, no. Say no more on this, I beg you."

What might have happened then Seg never knew.

A hail from aft brought their attention to Obolya scuttling out from his magnificent cabin, screaming, and his guards yelling, and Khardun and the Dorvenhork stringing their bows. An air of grim tension fell upon the boat.

Up from aft, paddling at high speed, foamed a long lean craft, a schinkitree with many paddlers, and flags, and a group of prijikers in the bows with their ramp ready to drop, ready to roar charging over in a welter of steel and bronze.

Those stem-fighters clustered in the bows looked hardy, tough men, clad in armor, their blue and white feathers waving. When the ramp went down and clawed into the stern of Obolya's boat, those prijikers would leap across like leems. They knew their business. Not one would fall into the brown, jaw-ravening water, not unless he was shafted through.

Obolya jumped onto the curved stern waving his arms and shrieking. The pursuing boat surged nearer.

Seg took up his Lohvian longbow and bent it with the practiced ease he had known since early childhood.

Milsi put a hand to her breast, staring wide-eyed aft. The paddlers along each side of the boat dug deeply, frantic with the lashes of the Whip-Deldar upon their naked backs.

From the boat aft of them a giant voice roared.

A Stentor, using a curly horn from one of the cattle animals of the plain, bellowed commands.

"Steer for the bank! Do not resist! Resistance is useless."

Seg, about to spit out in his bluff way: "We'll see about that, by Krun!" stopped, the words unformed.

The cluster of fighting men in the bows parted. The prijikers moved aside. Clearly to be seen the snout of a varter showed, aimed at Obolya's boat, and in the trough of the ballista there would be a large and heavy rock. Once the ballista clanged and the arms sprang forward and the varter disgorged that rock. . . .

"We shall be holed! We will sink!" gasped Milsi.

Obolya shrieked again, and his personal guards lowered their bows. Once the boat was holed and sank, the jaws lurking in the muddy waters would feast . . .

"There is no chance, my lady," said Seg. He looked at his bow. He looked at the pursuing craft. He saw the varter and pictured the cruelly sharp and heavy rock positioned in the trough. Carefully, he unstrung his bow. He took the string right off. He coiled it neatly and laid it away in his belt pouch. Then he took up one of the compound reflex bows, and put that dorven bow close by his hand.

Milsi said, "The guards of Kov Llipton will not be deceived, Seg."

"Nevertheless, I can but try." And he put the great Lohvian longbow down, pushing it half under the landing ramp, so that it looked a mere lump of wood.

Without orders, for there was need of none, the helmsman headed for the near bank.

Zim and Genodras threw down their glorious mingled lights, streaming in long swaths of ruby and jade. The breeze brought the scents of the plains, sweet grasses, dust, and the sky washed a pearly blue high above. The prow of the boat touched the bank, and she slewed and so came to rest in a ferny brake. The pursuing boat ranged up alongside, and the Stentor's voice roared forth again.

"Hold fast all! You are renders and will surely die!"

Willy-nilly, Seg and his comrades, menaced by drawn-back bows, watched as the guards poured into their boat.

# CHAPTER THIRTEEN

## Trylon Muryan

"If," said Seg, "we cannot cheat, contrive or fight a way out of this stinking dungeon, we are not fit to be called paktuns."

The dungeon itself, sunk into the ground, iron-barred, stank. Outside, at a higher level, the guards prowled. Some guards wore brown and white feathers, and for every guard with the brown and white, another guard wearing the blue and white paced him and kept him company.

Hundle the Design explained this.

"We are in the dungeons of Mewsansmot. This is Trylon Muryan's domain. But Kov Llipton, also, has jurisdiction, seeing that the town was the benefice of King Crox to Queen Mab when they were married."

"Fat lot of good that does us," said Khardun. "It means we have double the damned guards to deal with."

"Mayhap," said Seg, "we can start them fighting one another."

"Would the good Pandrite willed it!"

"I agree with Seg," growled the Dorvenhork in his grim Chulik way. He strained against the iron chains that bound him cruelly. "We are paktuns. You, Khardun the Khibil, are a hyrpaktun."

"That is so. We are not true to ourselves if we cannot burst a way out of here."

Seg refused to let the scarlet flames of horror into his brain—Milsi! What had happened to her? Where was she? What were these rasts doing to her now?

Of all the men, only Diomb had been sent along with the women. He and Bamba, Milsi and Malindi had been taken off. Seg could feel the passionate terror in him; and the ferocious coldness to push that away, and await what came, and to escape and shaft as many villains as needed shafting, and rescue Milsi and the others. . . .

"Seg! Brassud, dom, brassud!"

"Yes." At Khardun's comradely words, Seg did as he was bid and braced up. He could not go to pieces now, could not betray these men. The odd thing was, he thought, how they looked to him for guidance. Oh, yes, he had paid three of them good red gold to serve as hired paktuns. And the others took their lead from him. But, all the same, used as he was to command, and the giving of orders, he found this situation intriguing.

The little Och cleared his throat.

"Doms," said Umtig the Lock. "There is a way."

They all looked at him, chained in their misery in the dungeon. Umtig still wore the remnants of his finery, and the green-laced blue tunic was ripped only here and there. Seg could not see Lord

Clinglin, the tiny spinlikl, in his accustomed place about Umtig's breast.

The tunic moved of itself.

"Ah!" said Seg. And, then: "Can the little fellow do it?"

"Do it?" Umtig sounded mightily offended. "Have I not trained him assiduously ever since he was fortunate enough to come under my protection? Do it! You steer close to offending me, horter Seg."

"Then I crave your pardon, horter Umtig. And," Seg added, "by Diproo the Nimble-Fingered! Let him get on with it sharpish!"

Umtig jumped as though goosed. He bent instantly and started whispering fervently into the opening of his tunic. Presently a long prehensile arm emerged, the tiny but powerful hand grasped Umtig's ear, and with that as a purchase, Lord Clinglin climbed to Umtig's shoulder.

His large round eyes surveyed the dungeon. His small round head with the window's peak of darker hair giving him a religious look, a sweet and ooh-aahing look to soft-hearted ladies of the court, looked to the chained men in the dungeon oddly fragile to be the cunning object on which their hopes rested.

"Beautifully, now, my lord," whispered Umtig. "Sweetly now, as I have taught you. Away you go!"

Without hesitation, the tiny monkey jumped from Umtig's shoulder, clung to the iron bars of the dungeon, and then vanished up away out of sight.

Trylon Muryan Mandifenar na Mewsansmot held his title and lands at the hands of the king. King

Crox had made him, made his family, and took half of the goodness, produce and profit of the Mewsansmot estates.

Encamped a few miles outside the town on the fringes of the great plains where the ruffled rumps of uncountable head of grazing animals flooded the land with color and movement, Trylon Muryan lolled at ease. He was feeling pleased with himself. That morning he had ridden out on his mewsany, a strong and hard-mouthed beast called Black Thunder, and had successfully shot and slain two chavonths creeping among the herds. His crossbow had been placed among the trophies of the hunt. He had called Master Pumphilio, an artist of repute, to capture the moment and the glory in vivid paint.

So, there sat the trylon on his striped cushions of brown and white silk, sipping sazz, nibbling at miscils, awaiting the moment when he could repair to the dinner tent. These tents were more of the style of pavilions, peaked, striped with multi-colors, embroidered. Delicious aromas from the cooking fires where his slave chefs labored filled his mouth with saliva. He drooled at the coming repast.

Around him his chiefs, his major domo, his slaves, his Chail Sheom—pearl-ung, gauzy of garments, painted of face, and chained—waited on his every word, his every gesture. He was a man pampered in this life.

He ate gluttonously. He ate hugely. Yet he remained trim and dapper, with a figure that could still be spanned by a woman's outspread hands. And there were women aplenty who sighed to perform that divine function.

As he said, soulfully, it was a great pity and a wonder under the heavens of Zim and Genodras, that the great and glorious Pandrite had seen fit to take away his wife and his twins, and to cast them beneath the iron-rimmed wheels of a common Rapa's garbage cart.

So it was that when the zorca-rider appeared, dust-stained, bearing the marks of hard-riding, the trylon was prepared to treat him with great solicitude.

"Wine for the messenger." And: "Take your time, tikshim." And: "I am for the dinner table, so do not delay me at your peril."

The messenger gasped out his news, fragile, pallid, in mortal fear of this elegant man in the lounging robes trimmed with silver lace.

"The devil you say!"

Trylon Muryan sat up straight on his cushions.

He snapped his fingers, and his grand chamberlain scurried to do what was unspoken but necessary. Muryan sat deep in thought and then snapped pettishly at the messenger.

"You say they will be here in two burs?"

"Assuredly so, pantor."

"Very well. Get out."

The trylon sat again in thought. On his sallow face graced with a thin strip of chin beard of a dark color that was not a genuine black until it was dyed, a look of growing wonder curved his thin and painted lips. He began to throb with the wonder and the glory of what had happened. He knew, as Lem was his master and guide, he knew he had been appointed, anointed, chosen and selected.

"It must be!" he said, gobbling over his words, to San Frorwald. "The gods shine on me, and Lem is to be praised above all others!"

"You are undeniably in the right," said San

Frorwald in his grating voice. He was a Sorcerer of the Cult of Almuensis, a glittering and imposing figure, such a sorcerer of flash and presence as would be employed at the table of Trylon Muryan. San Frorwald glistened in a robe of green and gold and blue, tall of spiral-bound hat, imposing of look, a thaumaturgist of considerable powers. His beringed hands stroked the book chained to his waist. That hyr lif was gem-encrusted, and bound in the skin flayed from a newly slain maiden.

This sorcerer was the only confidant admitted to the secret thoughts of Trylon Muryan Mandifenar na Mewsansmot.

"Prepare everything," he told his major domo. "Nothing must go amiss, or your head is forfeit."

The major-domo, a butter-pated Gon, bowed, and acknowledged the command, and went to oversee the preparations. The Gon, one Nath the Keys, knew the trylon's threat was no idle one.

"Now the great and glorious Lem smiles upon me!" declared Trylon Muryan. "Now shall the brown and silvers see such a day as this kingdom has never before witnessed!"

The approaching cavalcade of whose advent the messenger had warned was observed, and escorted into the trylon's camp with great pomp. A full regiment of lancers preceded the column, their mewsany mounts hardy animals of the plains tamed to men's use. The carriage was covered with a yellow and green awning against the midday glare of the suns. Slaves with water jugs threw handfuls of water against the carriage to cool it and the occupants within. Feathers waved. There was a full regiment of mewsany cavalry to bring up the rear. In the midst of the glittering host rode the

principals, gorgeously clad, riding zorcas, those
supreme saddle animals whose hooves splintered
the light from burnished silver, whose spiral horns
were wound with gold wire. Stentors blew their
brazen trumpets in fanfare after fanfare.

Trylon Muryan, resplendent, walked out of his
pavilion to greet the arrivals.

The cavalry opened out to left and right. The
mewsanys of these two regiments were blacks and
grays, hard of hoof, pawing the ground as their
riders gentled them into the required positions to
take up their guard stations. Pennons fluttered.
The carriage rolled to a standstill before Trylon
Muryan's pavilion. He felt conscious of himself,
of the suns beating down, of the sound of the
cavalrymen, of the jingle of bit and bridle. He
could smell the dust off the plains, and scent the
savory dishes cooking in the kitchen area. He
swelled with the importance of the moment.

Being the man he was, he swelled with his own
importance.

Being the man he was, down he went, plump,
into the full incline before the carriage. His nose
dug into the dust of the plains, his rump stuck in
the air, he abased himself to all outward seeming,
and joyed in it, knowing the inner secrets of his
own heart and the fecundity and glory of the
schemes hatching there.

"Do rise, Trylon Muryan. Lahal."

He lifted his head, staring up.

The queen looked glorious, clothed in light,
glittering with gems, seen from this humble position like a goddess rising supernal into the air.

"Lahal, majestrix. Lahal. You are more welcome than—"

"Very probably. I have ridden out particularly to see you, trylon. Let us go into your tent where we may talk privately."

A frantic scrabbling followed as men and women jostled out of the way, making attempts to maintain protocol, pushing lesser wights clear, shoving to make a passage for the queen and the trylon.

Within the coolness of the tent Muryan swept a beringed hand about the displayed wealth and luxury.

"All I have is yours, majestrix."

Slowly she removed her dust-veil, the shamil of fine blue gauze hemmed with diamonds and seed pearls. Her brown eyes regarded the trylon meaningfully.

"That is so, Muryan. You hold your life at the hands of the king my husband. And he has given Mewsansmot to benefit me. I am glad you do not forget."

Muryan put a hand to his lips. He knew nothing of this woman. She had appeared suddenly, brought at the king's orders from Jholaix. She was the last representative, as far as the wise men knew, of the royal line in the vital female descent. She had been married to the king in a hasty, candle-lit ceremony in the palace of Nalvinlad. The moment the final words had been spoken the king had departed, paddling down the river to go on his fatal expedition into the Snarly Hills. The queen had waited no time at all before setting off after King Crox.

And, now, here she was, back and alive, and of a sudden promising to be an unexpectedly formidable opponent.

"How may I serve, you, majestrix?"

"In two things, which must be done immediately."

"Of course."

"One. You will send for my daughter, the lady Mishti, from wherever she has been banished. You will do this thing now. Your head will answer for her safety."

Muryan bowed that head that, on a sudden, seemed to him to be not so securely affixed to his neck. He rang a golden bell and his Relt stylor sidled in, pale feathers dusty and ink-stained.

"Send for the queen's daughter, the lady Mishti. Send Jikdar Parndan and his regiment. Bratch!"

The Relt bratched, quiveringly.

"And, majestrix?"

Before she could answer, Muryan rattled on: "Please, majestrix. A chair. Sit down. May I offer you wine, parclear, sazz?"

She waved a hand bare of any rings.

"Later. I am not well-pleased that you took it upon yourself to send my daughter away from Mewsansmot. One might think you sought to imprison her. I am well aware of her importance."

"Majestrix! I sought to protect her. Kov Llipton has designs—"

"I will come to that later."

"As you command."

"You and Kov Llipton do not see eye to eye. For every soldier he has wearing the blue and white, you employ one wearing the brown and white. If your mutual hatred flared into open conflict . . ." Again she made that small dismissive gesture. The shapeliness of her hands fascinated Muryan. She was a shapely woman altogether, the formal heavily embroidered and gold-laced gar-

ments barely concealing the proudness, the lissom-
ness, of her body. Yes, decided Trylon Muryan,
his schemes would involve pleasure as well as
profit.

"The other matter of importance, majestrix?"

"I came upriver in a boat belonging to a certain
animal-trader, Obolya Metromin the Zorcanim, under the protection of paktuns."

"I am overjoyed you were able to hire loyal
men."

"Ah, yes. It was not exactly a question of
hiring the paktuns. My desire to see my daughter
caused me to leave them under the protection of
one of your officers, a Jiktar called Harmo ti
Pallseray."

Muryan nodded.

"A good man. Loyal. He will do his duty."

"So I trust. First, I wish that Obolya be afforded every facility in the trading he carries out
here. Second, I wonder if you recall two others of
your officers—Hikdars Northag and Pafnut?"

He frowned and then he smiled. "I know all the
Jiktars who command my regiments, majestrix, of
course. But, as for the Hikdars who command the
pastangs within the regiments, well—" He spread
his hands, and the massed rings glittered. "Well,
majestrix, no, I do not know all of them. But
Hikdar Pafnut, I recall, yes, him I remember."

"Well," she said, and she made it brutal. "Both
of the rasts are dead, and may they rot on their
way down to the Ice Floes of Sicce."

"Majestrix?"

She told him what had occurred in Master
Jezbellandur the Iarvin's weapons bazaar. "These
men, your officers, Muryan, attempted the queen.

They were slain by my protectors. Therefore, no charges can possibly be leveled."

Muryan screwed up his face. "I agree, majestrix. But, Kov Llipton will not see the matter in that light."

"And you have nothing to say on the conduct of your officers and men?"

He saw his mistake.

"It is an outrage, majestrix! Of course—I shall have the matter thoroughly examined. Rest your mind. As for your paktuns, I feel sure Kov Llipton will pardon them."

She stared at him for a moment, not much caring for what she saw, yet knowing she had to use this man, for her own resources in this strange land where she had been made a queen in the game of power politics were parlous slender.

"You are frightened of the kov, Trylon Muryan?"

He blustered. "Frightened? Assuredly not, majestrix. Yet he is the man your husband gave the overlordship of the country to when he went away. His death grieves us all; also, it leaves Kov Llipton in a position of great power."

"That I see."

For the moment there was no more that could be accomplished. Muryan issued the necessary instructions.

She sat down. She put a hand to her forehead, and then, firmly, said, "Now I will take a glass of parclear, if you please, trylon."

# CHAPTER FOURTEEN

## Concerning Seg the Horkandur's discovery

Executions carried out in the provinces along the Kazzchun River were matters of elegant if bloody simplicity.

There was, quite obviously, no need to keep an executioner with an axe on the payroll. Prisoners due for the chop were merely invited to take a little swim in the river.

Reflecting on this, Nath the Keys shoved his bent back more comfortably against the straw-filled sack against the guardhouse wall, scratched under an armpit, flicked away a couple of pesky flies, and then took a chunky bite out of his cheese pie. As he was an apim with only two hands, these actions had to be performed in sequence, unlike those diffs with usefully more than two hands who'd do the whole lot in one go, and wipe their noses into the bargain.

The new prisoners stuffed down into the sink-hole under iron bars were very quiet. They, too, must be reflecting on the manner of executions along the river. Down the passageway with its barred cells at either side where less important prisoners were confined a dolorous series of wails and cries, pleas—and singing—broke the stillness of the night.

"Shaddap!" yelled Nath the Keys, spraying bits of cheese and pastry. The noises did not diminish. He had a party of drunks in there, a couple of fellows who'd robbed a Lamnia of his purse and been taken up by the trylon's guards, a fellow who had commented unfavorably on the trylon's personal habits in a too-public place, and an idiot boy and girl who'd stupefied themselves on caff and staggered doped and dazed into the temple.

Much as Nath regarded Trylon Muryan as an out-and-out bastard, there was still no call for Kov Llipton to come raging up here with his own men to take charge of the prisoners. The queen had said, quite distinctly, that the paktuns were not to be imprisoned, that the deaths of the two Hikdars and the men could be explained. Jiktar Harmo ti Pallseray was a bit of a ninny; but he could obey orders. And then Kov Llipton had arrived like a monster from the brown river itself, and changed everything.

On a board fastened to the wall the keys to all the cells and dungeons hung on rings. Nath the Keys, sitting against his sack, did not notice the tiny spidery hand reaching out from the shadows. Not a single key chingled. He took another bite from his cheese pie, beginning to worry if his lady love, Nardia the Yellow, really was, or if she was just trying to play him along for more cash. If she was and she wanted to, she could go along to Kov

Llipton and. . . . A drop of sweat rolled down Nath's nose and dropped onto his cheese pie.

A tiny grating noise came from the bars of the dungeons. Nath half-smiled. Poor devils. They were going for a swim. Once Kov Llipton got his teeth into you, you were as good as dead.

As this thought flitted through his head, one of the kov's soldiers walked in, a hairy Brokelsh with his blue and white feathers flaunting about him. Nath looked up.

"We're off for a wet, Nath. Nothing more doing tonight, and, by the Resplendent Bridzikelsh, this place would make a fish thirsty."

Nath eyed him a trifle warily.

"If that's all right with Deldar Stroikan. All I have to do is lock 'em up and feed and water 'em—if they're here long enough."

The Brokelsh did not take this too well. He put a hairy hand to the silver mortil head at his throat. Among the string of trophy rings in his pakai gleamed no less than two gold rings. A man of some repute, then, this Bandlar the Spear. He had slain two hyrpaktuns in personal combat, and taken from them their golden pakzhan rings to add to his pakai collection. Still, slaying a hyrpaktun did not automatically make you a hyrpaktun. That high honor was far more hardly won. Bandlar the Spear was an ord-Deldar.

"I've given Deldar Stroikan his instructions. If he and his audo cannot do the job for a bur or two while we clear our throats, then what is the world coming to?"

Nath was far too canny—and, if the truth be told, more than a little frightened—to make any scathing remarks about the white and blues coming up here and lording it over the brown and whites who were the inhabitants.

A clatter of iron on stone heralded the entrance of Deldar Stroikan. He showed in his flushed face the anger Nath had contained. His left fist gripped onto the hilt of his sword. As a so-Deldar, he was five steps below Bandlar the Spear in the grade structure within the Deldar rank. His pakai showed all silver; it was lacking gold, and it was shorter, a lot shorter, than the pakai dangling so insolently from Bandlar's shoulder.

"Yes, Deldar?" Bandlar's coarse Brokelsh voice conveyed insultingly his position.

As Nath could see, clearly for the sake of explaining his arrival, Stroikan jerked his right thumb at the pile of weapons stacked into a corner.

"The Jiktar will want every one o' those weapons strictly accounted for."

Bandlar simply swept aside the opening gambit in a positional tussle. "Make it so. And, I've looked. Most of the stuff is Krasny work. Those paktuns we've got stuffed down the sinkhole had better crafted kits. But, as for that great bar of iron one of the onkers carried—what paktun in his right mind would lug that about?"

"It's supposed to be a sword."

Nath ventured to chip in.

"I believe it's ceremonial. He probably stole it from the retinue of some noble, maybe even some king in his wanderings."

"Then he's a worse onker than I thought."

Bandlar the Spear stalked off, and after Stroikan so far forgot himself as to make a face at Nath the Keys, he, too went off to the guard positions to check his men. Nath was left alone to get on with his cheese pie.

So he thought.

A slithering grating sound from the sinkhole again made him give that half-smile through a mouthful of cheese pie. He could feel sorry for those poor devils. He did catch just the one astonishing glimpse of a shadow where the tallow dip could throw no shadow from anything he knew of in the guardroom, then the black cloak of Notor Zan fell on him.

Khardun said: "You needn't have knocked him cold, Dorvenhork. Now we cannot question him."

"Better safe than have him screaming his fool head off."

The others crowded in silently. Umtig felt bloated with pride. He glowed. Lord Clinglin had carried off his part with meticulous and wonderful skill, returning with the keys and making only a single tiny chingle of noise. Now Umtig and the spinlikl wrapped around his neck could let the big hairy fighting men get on with their parts.

Seg found their weaponry piled in the corner.

Each man took up his kit, some with a little grunt of pleasure, some with a feeling of relief. Seg turned the pile of other prisoners' weapons over, picked up the great Krozair longsword, and could not find his Lohvian longbow.

Probably that was still pushed safely under the landing plank in Obolya's boat.

He contented himself with one of the compound reflex bows, and took up two quivers of the shorter arrows. He looked around.

"Right, fanshos. Shaft anybody who tries to

stop us. Go more silently than the White Wind that
glides across Wistith Waste.''

On their way here they had been blindfolded.
Now they crept silently along the passageway and
heard the drunken discordant songs foaming from
the cells. Other voices joined in, yelling for the
drunks to shaddap, and so Seg, without a smile,
nodded his men on, confident they would not be
heard.

The passageway was ill-lit, the barred cells pools
of darkness. Seg discarded the idea of releasing
the drunks, for although they would create a fine
disorder, they would alert the guards far too early.
He passed the iron bars of a cell and a voice,
hoarse and raspy with wonder, said: ''By Zim-
Zair! How came you by that sword?''

Instantly, so fast his feet seemed barely to touch
the stone floor, Seg leaped at the bars. He peered
into the darkness. He said, ''Is that you, my old
dom?''

A man clad in a tunic that had once been white
moved toward the bars of his cell so that a single
vagrant gleam from the tallow dip on the opposite
side caught and etched his face. He had black hair,
very curly, and ferocious black moustaches brushed
arrogantly upward. He looked a wild and raffish
fellow, and he stared at the sword across Seg's
back with a hunger that tautened all the ridges of
his face.

He spoke. Some of the words he said were
ordinary understandable words, but what he was
saying was completely unintelligible to Seg.

At last, the leaden feeling banished from his
limbs and the dryness from his throat, the sawdust
from his brains—for he'd thought it was, he'd

really thought it was!—Seg said, "I am sorry to disappoint you. I am not a Krozair. This sword belongs to a friend of mine and I keep it in trust for him."

"By the disgusting diseased liver and lights of Makki-Grodno! This is, indeed, a marvel. I had not thought to find a single soul in this heathen place who knew of the Eye of the World."

Seg well understood how the people of the Eye of the World, the inner sea in the far continent of Turismond, believed themselves to be the center of the world, and all the enormous oceans and continents about them merely the frame.

"I am well enough acquainted with the Krozairs to believe that if I release you from this cell, I may entrust the safety of this longsword to you, as a Krozair brother."

"You may. I am called Zarado. Llahal—"

"I am called Seg. Llahal. Now let us get you out of it and a bash a few skulls and so escape free."

Khardun called back on a whisper: "Someone comes."

The drunks made enough noise to cover what followed.

Ten men, led by their Deldar, marched down the passageway, a full audo of soldiers. Their brown and white feathers frilled above their bronze helmets. These were the men who would hurl Seg and his comrades into the Kazzchun River. Shafts flew. Blades rose and fell, punched past corselet rim and withdrew, darkly stained.

The Deldar went down with all the famous Bells of Beng Kishi ringing in his head. When he recovered he was pinioned, and his men were mostly dead or unconscious. Seg glowered down, hands on hips, his face like a thundercloud.

"You, Deldar. You will answer a few questions."

Deldar Stroikan said: "You're all dead men."

"I think not. Not yet. But you do understand that you will be? Very good. Now, Deldar—where are the ladies who were taken up with us, and the dinkus?"

"This will not do you any good, you rast. You have slain too many of the trylon's men to—"

Seg put his face close into the Deldar's face. He could smell the man's wine-soaked breath, and, no doubt, his own onion-smell was spreading nicely in return.

"The Lady Milsi! If you don't answer, *now*, I'll slit your gizzard up, down and across! Where is the Lady Milsi?"

The man looked nonplussed at this. He licked his lips. "I heard that. The king is dead, and all the people with them. The Lady Milsi died, too, in the Coup Blag. Only Queen Mab returned safely, and she has gone to the trylon."

Seg heard this and did not understand it. It was not the same degree of non-understanding he had experienced with the Krozair. He shook his head to stop the ringing and said, "You are mistaken. The queen died in the Maze. We brought the Lady Milsi out safely. Now, you rogue, tell me—"

"I've told you!" The Deldar's eyes widened. It was clear he was dealing with a madman. "The queen was brought ashore with you and your band of cutthroats and rode out immediately in a great cavalcade to see Trylon Muryan."

"Trylon Muryan," growled the Dorvenhork, "is the man who put us down the sinkhole."

"And who threatened to throw us into the river." Khardun wouldn't forget that in a hurry.

Seg would not admit that ice flowed in his veins. He would not admit that a clutching hand gripped his heart with crushing force. He found it damned difficult to catch his breath. And his legs were shaking, he had to admit that, curse his stupid betraying legs though he might.

Lady Milsi—Milsi—was the queen. No doubt of it.

"So they mewed her up in chains and dragged her off to be thrown down before this damned trylon? HEY?"

"No, no. It was not like that. She was received with great honor and joy that she was still alive."

There was no doubt, no doubt at all, that Seg felt as though some gigantic oaf had kicked him in the guts.

"We will have to get moving," said Khardun. Then, in his Khibil way, he added: "I own I am disappointed in the Lady Milsi. But, queens are queens and have their own ways of dealing with us ordinary folk."

The Chulik thumbed up a tusk. "Ordinary folk, Khardun? And you a Khibil?"

"You know that I am not a king, not even a noble, Dorvenhork. But I think our friend Seg has been shrewdly struck."

"Aye. So let us get out of here, by Likshu the Treacherous!"

"What shall be done with this Deldar?" demanded Rafikhan.

"Oh—just thump him gently behind the ear."

This was done. Seg took no notice. Surrounded by the others, who now included the Krozair,

Zarado, among their number, he was more conveyed along the passageway than going as an understanding member of the escaping party.

They encountered no more guards, of either blue and white or brown and white allegiance, and so burst forth into the starry night of Kregen, out under the golden roseate light of the moon sailing above the town and the treetops—She of the Veils.

Just for the moment, Seg Segutorio, known as the Horkandur, didn't much care about anything at all.

# CHAPTER FIFTEEN

## Kov Llipton

"By Mother Zinzu the Blessed," exclaimed Zarado, "I needed that!"

He wiped the froth from his lips with a scrap of once-yellow linen. Seg's heart warmed to the Krozair. How many times he had heard that heartfelt expression!

Khardun and the Dorvenhork were still on speaking terms, and were sharing a bottle companionably. The others had their bottles and tankards on the sturmwood table, and the slaking of thirsts went on at a prodigious rate.

About them the noise of the tap room of The Aeilssa and the Risslaca flowed on in a muted fashion, for it was late and most of the fisherfolk had already left. The few farmers had gone long ago and only the merchants and the mewsany handlers seemed to have time to spend to sit and drink past the hour of dim.

"This is all very well," said the Fristle, Naghan

the Slippy. "But surely we cannot stay here long? The guards will be—"

"Of course they will," Khardun said with his expansive cocksure attitude. "But they have to find out that we are flown. Then they will set up a hue and cry. By then we'll be well out of it."

"If I may venture to ask," said the Relt stylor, Caphlander, in his usual nervous and apologetic manner. "Where we will go to be out of it?"

"Ah," said the Dorvenhork. He did not polish up a tusk; but his small piggy eyes glanced about the tap room. "That is the question."

"If you think," Hundle the Design lowered his tankard, "that we can march over the Mountains and reach North Pandahem—forget it. It'll be down the river for us."

"And you would steer us?"

"If we find a boat, doms, why, yes, of course."

Sitting with his nose in a tankard, Seg took little interest in all this. He was not going to allow himself to become maudlin over a woman. That the woman used to be Milsi, and was now the queen—this famous Queen Mab—merely made his resolve the stronger. These women looked to him. Quite apart from the gold he'd paid out, they sensed in him the qualities necessary for leadership. Well, by the Veiled Froyvil! he'd lead them down the river and out of this hell hole.

And yet—and yet!

He had really believed there was a future with Milsi. They had both been shafted by the same bolt of lightning. He was sure of that. He had known it with all his consciousness, known it unfailingly. Because she was a queen she had betrayed him, left him, consigned him to the dungeons. She had used him, had gained her ends, and then she had abandoned him.

No. He did not feel a happy man at that moment.

"One thing is sure," he said, his voice heavy and leaden. "We are all wanted men. There is a price on our heads, mark me on that."

"Aye. So we defy these rasts, and sail, we go downriver with Hundle the Design as our boat master—"

"That is true, Khardun," interrupted Rafikhan. "But Seg the Horkandur is our Jiktar."

No one argued that.

None of them offered much information about past lives. They did not volunteer information on their homes, what they had done, what seen, where adventured. Only Hundle and the Och thief appeared to own the Kazzchun River as home. What Umtig had done to land up in prison was obvious; the Relt stylor offered no information. The Fristle once mumbled a few words about a broken bronze plate and a death of a ninny; but that passed without comment. Truth to tell, Seg no more worried about the past misdeeds of this happy little band of fugitives then he fretted over the future mayhem they might cause. Nothing much made sense or reason or was of interest to him right now.

The supposed racial enmity between Rapas, Fristles and Chuliks did not seem to affect these representatives of their races, and Seg could feel a tiny twinge of relief that he had no worries of that tiresome nature. He wouldn't have cared had they flown at each other's throats as they might well have done in other circumstances. He felt the most important step he could take now would be to get himself well out of this stupid Kazzchun River business, get back home to Valka and Vallia. He'd find his old dom, and then they could set about putting the country straight for the last and final time. Then there were his Kroveres of Iztar to concern him. They had been abominably neglected of late, what with other priorities like Spikatur Hunting Sword. No, get out of this the quickest way he could and get off back home.

These new comrades of his might be rough paktuns or dubious characters along the river; they were sensible of the blow he had received, and while in no way expressing maudlin comfort, did not—as they would have done to a fellow sufferer— make mock of his affliction.

Seg stood up. "Let us go down to the riverbank and find ourselves a boat."

Hundle stood up, looking troubled.

"I mind me that the Law of the River does not take kindly to folk who steal boats."

Seg looked at him.

"The Law of S.O.N. takes precedence, Hundle."

Kregans love abbreviations and initials. Hundle lifted one eyebrow.

"The Law of Saving Our Necks. Right—wenda!"

Under the light of She of the Veils they crept down to the riverbank, and, by that streaming roseate golden light they witnessed a horrific scene.

A schinkitree had just pushed off, the long narrow boat laden with bales. The loadmaster had either not known his job or had botched it. The boat was sinking.

The paddlers chained to the benches screamed. They flailed their paddles at what reared at them as the water closed in. Horrible, macabre, disgust-

ing. . . . The monsters roared from the brown water,
churning it into suds, and those suds tinged omi-
nously red-black under the light. Huge jaws
crunched down. The boat slipped beneath the water,
dragging with her the doomed slaves. The free
men might just as well have been chained up.
They flailed and splashed and tried to swim, and
were engulfed. The noise of chomping jaws reached
across the water clearly to the bank. Seg half-lifted
his new bow, and then lowered it. Any help was
impossible. The men tipped into the Kazzchun
River were already dead men.

"We do not let that happen to us," he said.

Hundle let out a queasy breath. "The nightmare,"
he said, and he shook. "The nightmare!"

This distraction, gruesome though it was, gave
them the opportunity to find a boat at the downriver
end of the wharf, to untie her and climb in unseen.
They let her drift gently off downstream for a time
before taking up the paddles and driving her fast
and true through the treacherous water.

There was no pursuit they could see.

Fishing in the Kazzchun River was an occupa-
tion of an entirely different order from fishing in
other parts of the globe. You didn't just hang a
line and hook, suitably baited, over the side and
merrily haul in when you had a bite. Nor did you
spread out nets and haul them in, beautifully
freighted with the shining catch. If you did the
latter, you'd haul in mere shreds and rags. And if
the former—idiot!—you'd go headfirst over the
side.

One system involved placing two or three, even
four or five, boats alongside one another and deck-
ing them in. Then, secure behind barriers, the

fisher folk hurled long fish-spears. They had to
watch for their targets, and select the edible from
the predators. A flashing cast, the cruel barbs,
fashioned probably from the fangs of the very
monsters who lurked in the water, biting in and the
quick hauling in of the line. If you hung about
during that stage you'd most probably haul in only
half of your catch.

A river can support many different species, and
the fish and plants sustain each other. A rain forest
is a finely balanced biosphere, fragile, and living
things learn to live together and contribute their
part to the existence of the forest. Nalvinlad, being
situated near the end of the forest proper, partook
of the jungle and a little of the plains to the north.
Hundle expressed grave doubts that they'd escape
easily through the capital city without questions
being asked.

The Dorvenhork said in his growly way: "Let
us go ashore and walk, then. I am famished!"

They were all hungry.

"It would be best, if we are captured, not to be
found in possession of a stolen boat," counselled
Hundle.

Caphlander expressed the pious hope that all
would come well in the end.

In any event, the end appeared immediate and
sudden. A number of other boats and fishing craft
mingled along a broad reach, and from the tangle
of boats a paddler appeared thrusting along with
the brown water broken into cream-colored foam
at her prow. Seg looked and let rip with an exclamation of so profound a disgust no one else had
the heart to comment.

There followed a repetition of what had pre-

viously occurred. Their boat was forced to the
bank under pain of being instantly sunk. In what
seemed no time at all they were chained up and on
their way to Kov Llipton's dungeons in the city.
The speed of it all impinged only faintly on Seg.
His thoughts were not with him at the moment, not
fully, not so as to make him the Seg Segutorio
who would have put up a fight in his mad feckless
way—and probably got himself killed for his fool-
hardy pains.

The boat that had captured them had been sailing downriver, going along at a foaming pace, her
paddlers urged on by Whip-Deldars. She flew the
blue and white treshes, and the flags fluttered
brilliantly in the streaming radiance of Zim and
Genodras.

Kov Llipton looked down on his miserable band
of prisoners from his high deck aft. Cloth of gold
hangings framed his seat. His feet rested on a
balass and ivory stool. Watchful guards stood at
his back, waving long yellow feather-fans to cool
the Kov's brow.

Seg, chained up, looked at his own feet on the
deck.

"You are culprits, miscreants who have slain
soldiers in the execution of their duty. You are
drikingers. Therefore it is meet you should die
with the customs of the river."

Hundle said in an oddly dignified way in these
fraught circumstances: "No, pantor, no! We merely
protected defenseless women. We have done nothing to bring the Laws of the River upon us." It
was clear that Llipton's mention of these famous
laws had sparked Hundle the Design.

"Do not banter words with me!" The lion bellow roared about the prisoners. "I have judged. Now you swim."

Seg looked up.

Kov Llipton was a numin, a lion-man, with fierce whiskers and ferocious, lowering lion face. His mane gleamed brilliantly under the light of the suns. Robed in war harness, strong and robust like most members of his race, he glowered down, the lord, the arbiter, the final dispenser of justice along the Kazzchun River.

Seg's tongue crept out and wet his lips. He could deal with lion-men. He lifted his head, and his shock of unruly dark hair bristled.

"Listen to me, kov!" he bellowed out, and with every word his passion grew, his feelings of wrongness, his realization that good men should not have to die for sins they had not committed. "Listen to me, you great fambly, and learn the truth!"

Llipton hunched forward, suddenly. His massive pawlike hand gripped onto his sword hilt. He frowned.

"You speak to me—"

"Aye, you great ninny! I speak the truth!" Rapidly, not wasting a word, he shouted out what had happened in Master Jezbellandur the Iarvin's armory. At each sentence his comrades, with great venom, shouted out: "Aye!" and: "That is the truth!" and: "That was the way of it!"

During this the Krozair, Pur Zarado, joined in feverently. He knew a chance, slender though it might be, when he saw one.

Kov Llipton listened intently, waving away a guard who would have laid Seg senseless with a blow from his spear butt. Llipton's goldenyellow fur gleamed, his armor shone, his fierce lion-face bent frowningly down. Seg roared on, worked up, determined that he must do all he could to save the lives of his comrades. He forgot about the Lady Milsi as the woman who might have shared his life; she became the object in whose protection they had done what they had done and were now being persecuted.

"And so, Kov Llipton, you have the right of it now. If you condemn men for going to the assistance of ladies, of slaying rasts who attempt a lady and a queen, then your famous Laws of the River, aye! and of King Crox, are a blasphemy and a mockery in the eyes of honest men!"

The kov pointed.

"Bring that man up here to me!"

Seg was dragged forward and dumped down at the foot of the ivory and balass stool. He glared up and the malevolence in his face made the kov's eyelids twitch.

"If what you say is true—"

"If! I thought I spoke to a man of honor, who might recognize another such. Perhaps I was mistaken—"

"You are too proud and insolent, or too mad—"

"I am not proud, I hope I am not mad, and I am insolent only to a few people who deserve it."

Llipton brushed a beringed hand across his whiskers.

"I bear hardly on malefactors, yet I dispense a just justice. If your story can be proved. . . ."

"Ask Master Jezbellandur. Ask the queen."

"Believe me, that I will do." Llipton looked over the side. In a musing tone, he added: "That will not avail you, for by then you will have gone swimming.''

"Justice!" screeched Seg. He staggered up, his chains dangling about him. "What kind of justice do they teach you here in this Opaz-forsaken blot called Croxdrin?"

Llipton's hand stilled above his whiskers.

Seg saw that he had to bring this matter to a head by introducing an entirely new aspect to the situation. He drew a breath. He glared; but he got out what he had to say reasonably enough. "Let me speak to you, man to man, kov, or pantor, whatever they call nobles hereabouts. Maybe I can prevent a great misfortune falling upon you and all you love and value.''

"What are you babbling about now? Guards!"

Seg tried for the last time.

"You are all doomed, kov, you great fambly, if you do not listen to me!"

Llipton's hand resumed that stroking of his whiskers, and the rings flamed in the jade and ruby radiance. Then: "Drag him up to me. I will hear what he has to say further to condemn himself. Then he swims.''

Rough hands grasped Seg and hauled him up closer so that he stood swaying before the noble. Seg's face composed itself, the mad fey glare faded from those piercingly brilliant blue eyes. Even his shock of black hair seemed to settle and grow smooth. He drew himself up. He looked the kov straight in the eye.

"Listen to me, kov. You are a great noble here, and yet your poor barbarian people and your primitive river civilization are laughable. Know this! I am a kov. I am a Kov of Vallia! We in Vallia do not take kindly to anyone who insults one of us. I have an army at my command. Listen, I have already swum in your famous River of Bloody Jaws! I brought a voller down into the water—if you in your benighted ignorance know what a voller, a flier, is—and we swam to the shore and no monsters stopped us. My name is Seg Segutorio. These men with me are innocent of the vile charges brought—rather, you should send for a swim the perpetrators of the crime, if our justice had not already struck. If these men are not released then you must answer for the consequences when the might of Vallia is arrayed against you! Woe, indeed, on that day to all of Croxdrin along the Kazzchun River!"

For a space of time that stretched intolerably, Kov Llipton sat, gripping his swordhilt, brushing his whiskers, saying nothing.

In a voice soft as the kiss of steel, at last he said: "You claim much, Seg Segutorio. A kov? We shall see. Innocent? We shall find out. Insolent— ah, yes, you are that!"

Seg said nothing.

"One thing you claim, that you have already swum the river. That is the most difficult of all to believe—"

"And the least important. I am who I say I am. You may never have heard of Vallia—"

"Oh, yes. I know of Vallia."

Well, that explained the abruptly cautious attitude of the numim, then. . . .

"Take these men to the dungeons of the Langarl Paraido. Do not mistreat them. I will ponder the story, and have inquiries pursued. Until then, you tremble upon the brink of death."

"That," said Seg Segutorio, a Kov of Vallia, "is no new experience."

Suddenly, Llipton leaned forward. "I am prideful of my trust. I keep the Law for the king. You did not say, Seg Segutorio, of what lands you are kov?"

Seg didn't bat an eye or split a second. "Of Falinur. I have given the charge of my kovnate over to my comrade, Turko the Shield, while I visit heathen parts."

"Of Falinur—if it exists—I do not know. But I shall. Have a care, lest you—"

"What do you think can be worse, in your mind, than taking a swim in your river?"

"Ah!" said Kov Llipton, and waved his guards to take Seg back to his comrades. They had not been privy to what went forward upon the high dais; they were agog to know what the hell was going to happen next. All that Seg could do was to assure them that, at least for now, they weren't going for a swim.

With a treacherous feeling of pleasure, Seg realized he was feeling amused. These poor benighted folk in their jungly river! This proud puffed numim—who were a great race of folk, to be sure—and his bewilderment. Vallia! Ah, well, perhaps there had been a grain of truth in the tale Seg had spun. Enough, perhaps, to delay their swim by a few days . . .

# CHAPTER SIXTEEN
## In which Strom Ornol takes cover

The amusement Seg felt increased when the ruling came down from Kov Llipton regarding the due payment required. Whether the story was true or not, they had indubitably taken knives from Master Jezbellandur the Iarvin. Ergo—those knives must be paid for. Each member of the group was therefore scrupulously removed the price of one knife. Seg almost laughed.

"This has to mean our story is believed," declared Khardun. He gave his whiskers the first proper tweaking they had received in too long a time. "We shall soon be free."

"Before that we should escape," growled the Dorvenhork in his Chulik way. "By Likshu the Treacherous! Let us break a few skulls and make off."

"I am with you, Dorvenhork," quoth Rafikhan.

"Oh, and I, of course," said Khardun in his offhand Khibil manner. "Naturally."

They were immured in the dungeons of the

Langarl Paraido. The iron bars here were measurably thicker than those of the sinkhole in Mewsansmot. Also, they had a nice interesting habit here of sending condemned prisoners for their final swim wrapped in nets so that something could be hauled back and, if the head happened to be among the bits and pieces salvaged, then the heads of prisoners finished off by swimming could be impaled and exhibited along the city walls.

Of them all, Umtig would not be consoled.

He looked shrunken, his little puffed Och face miserable, his whole demeanor eloquent of the Thieves' own description—like a pickpocket with no fingers.

Lord Clinglin, amid much boisterous jocularity, had swung nimbly out through the bars, and Umtig had confidently predicted his speedy return with the keys.

Lord Clinglin had not returned.

Caphlander in his mild Relt way attempted to comfort Umtig. "Nothing harmful can have happened," he said, giving his beak a twitch. "And when we are released we will prosecute inquiries—"

"When? If!"

"So that," rumbled the dangerous Chulik growl, "is why we should break a few skulls and escape!"

"Yet," said Zarado, speaking up forcefully and yet in a smooth even tone, "there are other aspects. They are feeding us. They are not ill-treating us. And we believe they are sending to search out the truth of our story. We can escape now and look foolish—and once again be subject to the Law—if we are found innocent. Or we can bide a few days and see."

"Lull the rasts into a false sense of security," offered Rafikhan. "Aye, that is a good scheme."

The rest of them went at the argument and Zarado moved off to leave them to it. The cell was capacious and reasonably dry, and equipped with a few foliage-stuffed bags on which to sleep. The Krozair plumped down beside Seg, saying: "I owe you a deep apology, Seg—"

"Not so, Pur Zarado. It is I—"

"Listen. You gave into my charge the longsword. I no longer have the brand. So, you see how it is."

"The blade will return to its proper owner, never worry."

Zarado twisted up his ferocious moustaches, one side at a time. "I studied the blade. There were certain things upon it. And there were the letters DPKrzy. I knew a man once—Jak the Drang— who owned sword and letters similar—"

Without thinking through the implications, for the situation had clearly changed, and still embedded in the usual caution, Seg rapped out: "Oh that was old Duruk Pazjik."

"Of Pur Duruk Pazjik I do not know."

Fascinated by the past history suddenly opened out by Zarado's words, Seg had to say: "And this man, Jak the Drang?"

"Oh, he turned out to be the Emperor of Vallia. My comrade Zunder and I hired out for a time, then we drifted off, meaning to sail back to Sanurkazz." Here the Krozair heaved up a sigh. "I miss Zunder. We were parted in some heathen place called Molambo, and I was hired on to serve in swordships and so assisted in guarding boats up this Zair-forsaken river. I wish I'd never seen the place or this Grodno-Gasta of a Kov Llipton.''

"The Eye of the World is perhaps not so far as we think. The Chulik asked for huliper pie in a tavern—''

"Did he! The sailors of Magdag love that pie—''

"And he was accused of being in the army for it. Items of food and drink, recipes, fashions, travel widely.''

"Humph—that does not bring back our weapons or gain us our freedom, by the disgusting suppurating armpits of Makki Grodno!''

Seg shook his head, devoutly wishing that he could hear another Krozair brother saying these delicious oaths.

Shortly after that the guards came by and removed Seg from the cell. He was pushed along the corridors and into a room where guards wearing green and white waited. He squinted in the lamplight, for dawn was a few burs off yet.

"So it is the Seg the Horkandur I thought! Well met, comrade of the Maze!''

Strom Ornol, for it was he, strode forward with outstretched hand. His handsome, weak, aristocratic face did not look at all as Seg remembered it. Its habitual blot-like pallor was replaced by a crimson flush. A trimmed beard concealed the jaw. In fact, Seg had to look twice to reassure himself that this was the rast Ornol himself. The most astonishing thing was the broad smile on Strom Ornol's face.

Seg grasped the outstretched hand.

"I, Vad Olmengo, am come strictly charged with Kov Llipton's orders to bring you to him straightaway. Now, not a word! Not a word. Hurry!''

The guards with Ornol—or Olmengo as he had newly dubbed himself—closed up around Seg and casually and yet with purpose pushing the dungeon guards aside, swiftly escorted him outside. They pattered through the corridors, ascended to the surface, and mounted up on mewsanys waiting ready. In the first pale fingers of apple green and vermeil radiance they rode swiftly for the southern gate. No one spoke. The guards at the gate allowed them through when a Hikdar leaned from the saddle and rattled off orders from Kov Llipton. They cantered through and so entered onto the jungle trackway beside the river. The smells of forest and river mingled. The sound of the mewsanys, the clink of bit and bridle, the feel of leather and the ungainly clip-clop-clip of the six-legged riding animals might in other circumstances have lulled Seg Segutorio.

He remained quiveringly alert.

The weird friendliness of this blot, Strom Ornol, came as distinctly unsettling.

The circumstances of their parting, when the Lady Milsi—who was really this famous Queen Mab!—had told a few home truths and Ornol had reacted in his stupidly vicious way, forcing Seg to stick a knobby fist into his mouth, could hardly cause any friendly feelings. Ornol would in the normal way of the blot have him strung up or sent swimming. So. . .?

The track reached the riverbank with the massed trees receding to leave a small open space. Here a hut of rotting branches and tattered papishin leaves sagged over a wooden jetty. A boat was tied up, silent and waiting, with the boat master in his typical leaf hat standing shading his eyes. The cavalcade rode up and the guards dismounted.

"Can we talk now, strom?"

"Dismount, Seg the Horkandur. We go aboard the boat."

The guards in their green and white tied their mounts to leaning posts and began to board. Seg dismounted. Ornol—or Olmengo—drew his rapier. Four guards stood by him with bared swords. Ornol's smile changed.

"Step aboard, Seg—"

"What is this about, strom?"

"You call me pantor!"

The vicious haughtiness of the words was more in keeping with the Ornol Seg knew. The noble's expression changed. He was enjoying himself. He put up a beringed hand and ripped the false beard free. He rubbed a kerchief over his cheeks, and it came away reddened, and, lo! his face was the face of Strom Ornol, pallid, like the underbelly of a fish.

"Everyone will believe you escaped with the assistance of Vad Olmengo, who is a stupid adherent of Llipton's." The guards, too, were enjoying the farce. They ripped off their green and white feathers and replaced them. Seg saw the colors of the feathers they placed in their helmets.

Brown and white.

"You are a fool, Segutorio, and an insolent cramph! You are going swimming. Then we shall deal with Jezbellandur. There will be no proof against Trylon Muryan's men—and you will be dead and out of the way. As for your comrades, they are fish food as soon as your escape proves your guilt!''

Seg did not feel in the least horrified. He saw the boatmen had already cast off the rope at the prow of the boat and were holding her steady. Ornol motioned with his rapier.

''Step aboard, you rast.''

Obediently, Seg moved forward. They thought they were clever, yet they had not bound him. That wouldn't be necessary when he was threatened by so many swords. They'd just sail out into midstream and push him overboard.

Very well. . . .

''So you work for this fellow Muryan, Ornol?'' Seg talked casually, moving toward the guards and their swords, watching the storm.

When he moved he moved like a leem.

He hit the first two guards inside their swords. They toppled backwards, arms flailing. They screamed in mortal terror long before they hit the water. . . .

Ornol skipped backwards, yelling. Seg swiveled, sloshed the next guard so that he dropped, stunned. He ducked without a thought, turning again and sticking out his foot so that the fourth guard, rushing on and yelling in bold fury, tripped. That guard, screeching horribly, staggered on off balance and went splash into the murky waters.

''A madman!'' screamed Ornol. He jumped for the boat and scrambled over the gunwale anyoldhow, already screeching for his archers to loose.

The bowmen in the boat were not numerous; there were enough to feather Seg before he could reach cover. Seg had a deep respect for the power of bows. He saw the composite bows bending, saw five at least shafts aimed at him. He had the skill to deflect arrows, arduously taught him by the Bogandur, and could weave his way through an arrow storm—but he had no weapon with which to make the deflections.

Very well—he'd run for it, and dodge, and win free.

In that instant one of the bowmen jumped as though stung and clapped a hand to his eye. His bow clattered uselessly to the deck. Another archer whirled around a full circle, dropping his bow. When he faced Seg again there was something odd about his eye.

Seg put his head down and ran for the trees, jinking like a hunted animal, which he was.

A voice ripped from the trees.

"Seg! Over here! Run!"

Seg ran.

Two arrows plunked into the mud of the track before he reached shelter—then he was hurling himself head over heels into the trees and, already, was alert to the dangers of the forest.

He saw a small, lithe form, clad in an astounding rig of scarlet and gold, with green feathers waving, and a long tube at its mouth. Cheeks swelled to enormous balloons, and puffed—and the next dart sped.

"Diomb!"

The dinko did not bother to reply. Seg watched his amazing performance. As a bowman of some repute, Seg could judge and admire superb shooting.

Diomb's two upper hands held the long blowpipe in a brace. His other two hands withdrew darts from his magazine pouch and fed them in a steady stream into the mouthpiece of the ompion.

He drew, placed, and blew, drew, placed and blew. He sucked in his breath with whooshing open-mouthed gusto. Darts sped.

Seg tumbled down among the muck of the forest and turned, at last, to stare out onto the river-bank and see just what this dustrectium was accomplishing.*

Panic-stricken, the boatmen had cut the stern rope. The boat drifted out and downstream. Sundry splashings and churnings in the water indicated where the river was living up to its name with respect to those unfortunate wights who had fallen in. There was no sign of Strom Ornol. If Seg knew him, he was cowering well out of it, head down.

At last Diomb stopped shooting. The range opened out past the effective reach of the blowpipe.

"Seg!"

"I give you my thanks, Diomb, and the jikai!"

"I enjoyed that. It proves I have learned the ompion and can earn my hire as a paktun."

"You have and you may, may Erthyr be praised!"

Presently, when the boat, still without a paddler in sight, had drifted off, they stood up and walked out onto the wooden jetty. The guard whom Seg had stunned was about to recover his senses, groaning. Diomb put his little foot against the fellow's gut and started to push him into the water.

"Hold on, Diomb. We can't just kill the silly bastard like that—"

"Why not?"

"We-ell—"

"He would have killed you, and laughed doing it."

---

*dustrectium: firepower

"All the same, he is just a guard, earning his hire." Here Seg, admitting of no further argument, clouted the guard over the head again with his picked-up sword, and glared straight at Diomb, head down and jutting.

"I shall understand the ways of this preposterous outside world one day, I suppose, by Clomb of the Ompion Never-Miss!"

Seg looked around. "He has this sword and a knife, and that is all. Oh, well, that is better than being empty-handed. Now, Diomb, tell me all about it."

Abruptly the dinko suffused with passion.

"Of course! I was so enjoying this little fight I forgot. Seg! The Lady Milsi—"

"You mean Queen Mab." Seg's voice grated in a surly unfriendly rasp.

"Why, yes. I do not understand it all. Her name is Milsi. And it is Mab. But, Seg, that great rogue Trylon Muryan has her a prisoner! In a monstrous tower!"

"And I suppose the cramph plans to marry her and make himself king?"

"Seg! You do not sound as though you are Milsi's friend." Diomb stared up, his little face creased into a scowl of incomprehension. "Are you not feeling well? Perhaps you have an ache in the guts. . . ?"

"I've an ache, all right. If Milsi wants to marry this Muryan fellow, then that is her business. I must get back to my comrades, and Jezbellendur. If he is slain then a key witness vanishes. There is no time to waste—"

"There is no time to waste, true, Seg the Horkandur! I do not understand you, after all that you and the Lady Milsi were together! What ails you?''

Seg was already turning away and reaching for the best of the mewsanys. He grasped the reins looped around the standing post. ''Look, Diomb. Bamba is well? Good. Then you are all right. As for me, I am alone.''

Diomb scuttled across and his upper left hand reached up to fasten on Seg's muscle-corded arm.

''Listen to me, Seg! Milsi is imprisoned, with Bamba and Malindi. She sent me—I escaped, and a pretty piece of trickery that was, too—and she sent me to ask you. I followed this Strom Ornol, who takes his orders from Muryan, and crept through the jungle after you, and—''

''And you saved me, Diomb. I do not forget that.''

''But you must go to the Warvol Tower leading our comrades and rescue the ladies!''

''So Milsi turns to me when she is in trouble again, imagining I will come running like a little mili-milu when she rings her golden bell and wheedles and puts out a bowl of milk? Well, Diomb, my comrade, I have finished with that foolishness. When she marries Muryan it is sure that Malindi and Bamba will not be harmed, will be richly rewarded in the wedding party. As for me, time presses, and my comrades fester in a dungeon—''

''There is no time to bring your comrades if they cannot go at once! The wedding is planned—''

''Do not tell me! I do not care!''

Diomb stood there, face a single stricken question mark. He shook his head. He swallowed. He tried again.

''Lady Milsi is Queen Mab, and she holds you

in high honor and tender loving care, Seg. This is
so—"

"This is feathers from a zorca!"

Diomb let go Seg's arm. He jumped up and
down with frustrated rage. He started to yell.

"I don't know what is the matter with you, Seg
the Horkandur! You are no jakai! We thought, all
of us, only of you when misfortune fell on us!"

"Oh, aye, typical!"

"You are an ingrate! You are not deserving of
the Lady Milsi's esteem or affection, still less of
her love! After all she has done for you—"

"By the Veiled Froyvil, Diomb! You try me
hard!"

Then Seg paused. He took a trencher of a breath.
His chest swelled as only an archer's chest can. He
was not just an ordinary man, was Seg Segutorio.
He could feel the dinko's words like lashes upon
his spirit. But, there had to be more to this, there
had to be some spark of what he had felt still left
to him . . . He let the enormous breath out and he
said: "Diomb, my friend. Maybe I have the wrong
of it. Maybe—you spoke of Milsi's love. I have
received no sign of it, save for a foolish passing
moment soon forgotten. But, mayhap there was a
reason for the queen using us warriors to escort her
safely home, and then to have us dumped down
into a sinkhole and ready to go swimming in the
River of Bloody Jaws. Maybe this reason was not
the obvious one we believed—"

Diomb looked horrified. Then he jumped up and
down and almost fell over himself trying to sputter
his words out.

"I see! I see! You blame Milsi for putting you
in the dungeon!"

Still wrought up, Seg shook his head, his impatience wanting to brush aside stupid matters of
logic. "Well, not exactly. She did not put us in
the dungeon. But we were chucked down the sinkhole because we defended her, and she rode off as
a great queen and left us to fester!"

The look that crossed Diomb's face would have
made Bamba hug him with delight.

"You said, Seg the Horkandur, that mayhap
you did not have the right of this sorry business."
Diomb spoke in a light, easy way, a tone not
nonchalant or casual, but airy and rippling with
hidden amusement. He could be a little devil at
times, could Diomb the dinko.

"I said this. Go on."

"Then I have to tell you that you are an onker
with a head full of the fungus that sprouts on the
forest floor. Why do you think Ornol was sent by
Muryan to pick *you* out of the dungeons and throw
*you* in for a swim? Hey?"

"We-ell—"

"I suppose you imagined it was because you
were the leader, the most important, the high and
mighty puffed up pantor among us? Confess it, I
challenge you!"

"If I had been thought to have escaped, the
others would have received short shrift—"

Diomb gave a curt cutting gesture with his upper left hand. "I will tell you. This piece of
festering dung called Muryan wishes to marry Milsi
and thus hold title to the kingship—I have learned
all this. He knows Milsi loves you and he will
have you dead!"

"Do what?"

"You heard me, Seg the Horkandur!"

"You mean Muryan wants me dead, not Milsi?"

"Cretin!"

"Then—then what you say is true—there is danger for her—"

"She did not abandon you. She rode to seek her daughter and gave strict instructions you and our comrades were to be well-treated."

Seg glared around on the brown waters of the river, on the bank and the sagging shed, at the mewsanys, around to look unseeingly at the ranked dark green masses of the trees. Again he shook his head. He felt bloated, and yet shrunken. One thing he did know, without a moment's hesitation.

"I shall ride to the Warvol Tower. You must see to Jezbellendur and our comrades. One thing I know, Diomb—if Muryan does wed Milsi against her will, then it will be he who will be the dead man!"

# CHAPTER SEVENTEEN

## Seg Segutorio builds a bow

A slim paddler skimmed down the Kazzchun River passing without hindrance where any other boat would be forced to halt and declare occupants and contents. The schinkitree flew the flags of Croxdrin; but the tresh that gained this imperious passage flew from a taller mast than any other banner. This was the personal flag of Kov Llipton allied to the kingdom's messenger service.

Sitting on his comfortable chair in the stern, Tyr Naghan Shor brushed up his fierce whiskers and the streaming radiance of the suns glinted from his golden mane. Kov Llipton trusted folk of his own race to carry secret messages and discover intelligence of the river. The vague form of the Xaffer, squatting to one side, offended no one, for the Xaffers are a race strange and remote, and employed usually as secretaries and domestics. This Xaffer, Ninshurl the Seal, wore a decent blue robe girt with a silver chain, yet he was slave.

"A fool's errand, Ninshurl, I warrant you, by Numi-Hyrjiv the Golden Splendor!"

"Yet the kov was most insistent, master."

"Oh, one does not quarrel with Kov Llipton, not unless they wish to take a little swim. All the same, if the hulus of Mattamlad are mindful to be awkward . . ."

"We fly the flag of truce, master. They will listen to what we have to say."

"You are right, of course. All the same, I have left a most gorgeous numim maiden for this arduous duty, and I shall not waste too much time, believe you me."

The boat sped on downriver, driven powerfully by the hardened muscles of specially selected paddlers, slaves every one, chained to their benches.

Mattamlad at the mouth of the river slumbered under the suns. Here mud stank into the air, and the heat rotted everything. Tyr Naghan Shor under his flag of truce was allowed passage past the guard boats, for Mattamlad was an independent port town, and owed no allegiance to King Crox or his country to the north.

Reporting in at the bureau for foreigners, Tyr Naghan saw the tall masts of ships lying in the port area. He sniffed. He regarded the folk of Mattamlad with contempt; yet there was no doubt they were in more direct contact with other nations. Still, one day, all in Pandrite's good time, Kov Llipton would sweep down the river and annex all here.

"Your flag of truce and your letters will be honored, Tyr," the port official informed Naghan. "But I think it wise if you concluded your business within the space of a single day."

"I will if I can. But you know foreigners—"

"Oh, aye," said the official, a wizened marcer whose comb and side-brushes were much bedraggled, and whose curved body showed the effects of a long-ago swim—a quite inadvertent swim—in the river. For that miraculous escape he was known as Nath the Flounder. "Oh, aye, Tyr Naghan Shor. By the Bloody Jaws of the Brown River Herself, I think we know foreigners better than you."

Not allowing his natural numim authority to exert itself over a matter so petty, Naghan took himself off. He walked through the muddy street with a swing, judging that he would just get indoors before the rain fell down like a solid blow on everyone and everything. He passed the inns with a cock of his head at the sign of the Mermaid's Ankle, walked with the Xaffer at his side and rear, into a wider thoroughfare where a raised wooden sidewalk indicated the higher status of the neighborhood.

"There it is," he said, and strode on, turning up wooden steps to a bronze gate. A large house walled off stood beyond the bronze gate. At his ring a man answered the bell with a cheery remark and a genial presence. This man wore a buff jerkin over a tunic whose sleeves were banded in red and yellow. He wore two swords.

"Come on, come in, horter. I shall announce you at once."

Tyr Naghan grunted in a noncommittal way. As he entered, another man was just going out, walking fast to reach the nearest inn before the rains came. He wore a buff jerkin and buff breeches, and his hat possessed a wide rolled brim with a

jaunty feather curling at the side. He gave the
numim a cheerful "Llahal, horter," before trotting
off toward the taverns.

Tyr Naghan Shor, followed by his Xaffer slave
secretary, went into the building. As the doors
closed and the first drops of rain fell splat onto the
mud, he said: "A waste of time. Just a waste of
time."

The so-called "big" plains of northern Croxdrin
were extensive; but in no way could they be com-
pared to the enormous areas of Segesthes where
the wild clansmen rode on and on for week after
week and still there was no end to the plains.
Herds of animals grazed here, and the predators
had their fill during feeding time in the age-old
way. Seg rode a mewsany at breakneck speed, two
more tailing on the leading ropes, and he no longer
carried a sword.

Three quarters of the blade lay far back down
the trail embedded in the side of a wersting, and
the hilt rested a few dwaburs farther on, shoved
well and truly down the sharp-fanged gullet of the
leader of the wersting pack.

Diomb's directions had been precise. Seg knew
how much farther he had to go when he saw the
brown and yellow tents clustered about a stand of
trees breaking the level of the plain. He slowed.
The werstings were vicious hunting dogs, black
and white striped killers; but he had outrun them
now for the loss of his sword and two mewsanys.
What lay up ahead in those tents could be far
worse trouble.

He felt damned naked without a bow, by Vox!

He was tired, hungry and thirsty. None of that

mattered until he had taken Milsi and the others safely out of the clutches of Trylon Muryan. He'd eaten all the provisions in the mewsany's saddle bags. He kept religiously intact the last bottle of wine, a mediocre red stuff. The girls might need a refresher when he found them.

When the Maiden with the Many Smiles shone down refulgently in a pink wash of moonlight Seg scouted the camp and the Warvol Tower beyond. As for the tents, they housed simple herdsmen of the plains, who could ride their mewsanys with consummate skill, hurl a rope, cut and slash with their heavy halberd-like strangchis to drive off the werstings. Of bows they appeared to have only tiny self bows that wouldn't stick a woflo's hide.

As for the tower. . . .

The thing brought back vivid memories to Seg Segutorio of Erthyrdrin. Like a Peel Tower, it soared up, stark and brutal against the stars. There were no outworks. Set here to guard a long-forgotten frontier, it was now kept in use by Trylon Muryan to immure his prisoners. Similar towers, stark, simple, separate, had dominated the skylines of Seg's youth. Erthyrdrin might be vastly different from these plains, being a land of valleys and fey folk whose characters were yet shrewdly practical, yet it shared the architecture. The Warvol Tower lofted, tall, unpierced by any window or arrow slot for the first hundred feet. Above that the slits leered down. Near the top there were even trellised arcades supported on slender pillars. Here in Pandahem no thought was given to the defense against aerial attack. These people did not expect a host of saddle flyers to burst upon them from the clouds. They had not witnessed airboats swooping in to disgorge fighting men.

Seg had no saddle flyer. He had no voller.

All he had was a knife.

Diomb had said: "They are kept in the chambers with columns of blue and yellow. The columns of green and yellow are where the quarters for the guards are situated."

Staring up, Seg cautiously circumnavigated the tower. He assured himself that those columns up there *were* blue and yellow. If that blue was really green . . . Well, that lay in the hands of the all-seeing Erthyr of the Bow.

A ramp curled up from the ground three quarters of the way around the tower before reaching the main door. This was set at a cunning oblique angle in the masonry so that no room was afforded for the swing of a ram.

There was no way, Seg had to face the truth, that he was going to force his way in through that door and then up all the interminable stairs within to the prisoners' quarters at the summit.

He took himself off to the herdsmen's camp like a gray wraith, skulking like a lurfing of the plains.

He kept his saddle animals well away from those of the herders. He did first things first. Instead of stealing some food, he went off to the thickest part of the stand of trees away from the tents, and settled down to work.

Had he not had the fortune to be favored with the knife, he considered gravely, he'd have chewed the damned wood off with his teeth. . . .

To say that he could not remember when he had built his first bow was correct, for he seemed to have been building bows all his life; but he could well recall the very first adult bow. And, of course, there was the stave of the green Yerthyr wood he had cut from Kak Kakutorio's tree. The trees growing here in Pandahem now were not Yerthyr—most certainly not. The Yerthyr, of a green so dark as almost to be black, was lethally poisonous to animals without the special second stomach such as the thyrrixes of Erthyrdrin had. Well, even had these trees been Yerthyr there would be no time to fashion a real longbow in a single night. A longbow took four years or so. . . .

Around him within the trees of this wood lay staves and billets waiting to be released and freed into longbows. All he wanted was one decent stave, for he would not contemplate jointing two billets. Eventually he selected a limb in which the grain appeared to run straight and which had the slightest of curves so that he could compensate for the string-follow. His knife went swish-swish through the wood, smooth and gentle strokes that slivered the heart wood away with full respect to the lay of the grain. He found places where the grain forced itself up in a curve and so he left that curve there, rightly contemptuous of any stupid attempt to cut the sapwood to conform.

Above him the Maiden with the Many Smiles wheeled through the stars, and the Twins shed down their mingled pinkish light, streaming shadows between the trunks. Seg worked on, head bent, concentrated into a single organism that could do this thing superbly well.

Bowyers there might be in this world of Kregen; there were no finer builders of bows than those of Erthyrdrin. He carefully thinned the limbs of the bow, constantly checking with finger and thumb, with eyes that could judge to a whisker. A lifetime's experience was now coalesced into this one task, to make a bow that would cast aright.

Gradually the rough limb torn from the tree assumed a section something like a thimble. Stout in the handle, cunningly tapering to the tips. He would just have to cut string notches there, no horn or ivory nocks in this bow. Only two pins bothered him, and these he left with plenty of spare wood to be on the safe side. He was working at a pace that, to an observer, would appear cautious and steady and even slow. In reality he prepared and trued the bow with prodigious speed.

Every now and then Seg cocked an eye at the Moons. He checked the time, aware of the passing moments.

When he first tested the bow he used a bow-string from his pouch. At least that was proper, a real silken string from his own longbow. The bow bent sweetly and he held it up, muscles bulging, to see better the way the two limbs curved and to judge the arc. The sapwood on the back and the shaped heartwood on the belly worked together. He made a tiny clicking sound of satisfaction. The fistmele, the clenched fist and upright thumb, that measured the proper distance between string and handle was right. The bow felt right. The handle was a bit of a mess; no time to fix a real handle. Now for the shafts. . . .

In the end he had to settle for the heart of three leaves, cut down to long and narrow flights. He fastened the fletchings with a length of scarlet thread ripped from the edge of his loincloth. There was no need for a head.

He might simply have taken a suitable springy

branch and fitted the bowstring and tried that. But he felt that the cast ahead would demand length—or, rather, height—strength and accuracy. For a Bowman of Loh there was really only one way to secure those requirements.

"Now," he said, speaking softly and with great solemnity, "may Erthanfydd the Meticulous approve of this work and bless this newborn bow."

The final flourish remained. Dutifully, he cut his sign neatly into the wood without marring the finish. That sign he felt might help . . .

The feel of the bow in his hand was odd, of course, for very many reasons. The lack of seasoning would mean that the bow could never, in the opinion of a Bowman of Loh, be a proper longbow. As for the arrow, all his skill and judgment had to serve in getting the spine right, in seeing that the shaft was not too stiff or too weak for the weight of the bowstave.

He'd been forced to tighten everything up in this devil of a rush. And he was famished. Scouting around the herdsmen's tents he came across an abandoned bowl of cheese which, when he dipped his fingers in and sucked, tasted like King Golanfroi's Nosedrops—and every child knew what they tasted like. Still, he sucked down and didn't breathe in too hard through his nose. Then he reconnoitered the piquet lines and discovered the coil of rope he was after. The ropes were used between posts for temporary corralling purposes. With his booty over his shoulder he went back to his clump of trees.

Unraveling a fine strand took time. He'd made the distance judgment with the experienced eye of a shooter. He wouldn't be out more than the length of a man's body. When he had his fine long strand he coiled it with exquisite care and fastened one end to the arrow.

Then he picked up a splinter of wood, whittled the end to a needle point, and set off for the Warvol Tower.

The guards were not foolish or masochistic enough to stand a watch out on the open plain when no one was going to get into the tower but through the one doorway. Seg circled twice, checking, and then stationed himself under the spot where, high above and seeming to reel sickeningly against the stars, the blue and yellow arcade showed.

If that wasn't blue up there. . . .

Now was the time.

Quickly, he pricked the ball of his left thumb with the needle-sharp splinter and a drop of blood, black and shining, oozed out. With the other end of the splinter and in his own blood, he wrote on the leaf fletchings: "Haul in."

Sucking his thumb took no time. He gripped the bow. He held it familiarly, and yet with the tentativeness of fresh acquaintance. The bow felt good. Had he been using one of his own bows he would simply have lifted the stave, drawn and let fly. As it was, he felt his way into the shot, sniffing the faint night-breeze, feeling the waft of air on his cheek. He looked up and the bow followed him.

Seg shot in his bow. He felt the draw, the brace, the loose. The shaft sped upward. The fine twine unraveled at lightning speed.

The arrow soared up and up against the stars. It curved. It hovered. The twine whirled away aft, seeming to vanish where it neared the arrow. With the suddenness of all shafts in flight, the arrow vanished between two of the blue and yellow columns.

No lights showed through the slits above him, and only dimly seen a wash of radiance seeped around the columns. He waited. He held the slender thread in his hand. In only a few moments that stretched like the last day before paynight, the thread jerked in his hand. He jerked it gently three times and then watched as it began to draw away upward.

The check when the heavy rope came on amused him. Then whoever it was hauling in took a fresh purchase and the rope whistled up the sheer side of the tower.

He had judged well. There were perhaps five man-lengths left when the rope quivered and hung still. He waited for them to tie it off above, and pulled. An answering quiver reassured him. He put the bow down, laid both hands on the rope, and hauled hard. He pulled with determination to dislodge any shoddy knots up there. The rope held.

With that, like the little spinlikl Lord Clinglin, up he went. He climbed using his arms alone, hand over hand, only occasionally having to use his feet to fend off. Just below the arcade he paused. He was breathing deeply and evenly. Now was the time for a guard to smash him across the head with his sword, or more simply just to cut the rope. . . .

He struck his head over the edge.

Malindi, Bamba and Milsi stared at him as though he were a magician popping out of an empty chest.

"Seg!"

"Quiet."

He hauled himself in over the edge. There was no time to talk, to do anything but haul in the rope. When he had the end he grabbed Bamba, wrapped a bowline about her and pushed her off with a fierce: "Do not cry out, Bamba!" in her tiny ear.

She lowered down without a squeak.

"If Bamba can make no sound, neither will I," quoth Malindi, bravely. She was scared stiff.

The rope slackened off and then wriggled. Bamba had slipped out of the bowline on a bight and Seg hauled in. Malindi went down with her eyes fast shut, her heart in her mouth, damply—and without a sound.

"She is a brave girl," whispered Milsi. "I prayed you would come to rescue us, Seg, my jikai."

"Quiet."

He hadn't got over his feelings of abandonment just yet, unworthy though they were. He felt awkward in Milsi's presence, almost embarrassed.

Each woman had taken a few clothes and necessaries gathered up from the toiletry table. Milsi glanced about the room beyond the blue and yellow columns, and then, very firmly, slipped the rope about her. Seg payed out and down she went. Presently the signal rattled up and he had the reassuring knowledge that the three women were safely down. He took his sole arrow, stuck through his belt. He went over the side like a lizard sliding over a rock. Down and down and his feet hit the grass with a thump.

"Oh, Seg!"

"Talk when we are away."

Had the rope been dry enough he'd have set it alight to confuse those rasts up there. But it held dampness and so, with a feral look around that boded ill for anyone foolish enough to cross his path, he led off. The women followed silently, holding each other in mutual comfort.

They reached his three mewsanys. Here, immediately, a fresh problem presented itself.

"I could not ride, my lady!" Malindi clutched her thin tunic to her breast. "A saddle animal like the great ladies! Oh, no, my lady!"

Bamba said: "Perch on that great beast!"

Milsi said, with a sigh: "We were brought here in a carriage, Seg."

"I will take Malindi up on my saddle. You take Bamba. And be sharp about it. We must be well clear by dawn."

They jumped at his tone.

They did as they were bid and after a time they changed around and brought the third mewsany in to relieve the extra load. They rode silently, as Seg had enjoined.

The awkwardness persisted, exacerbated by his awareness that Milsi was not aware of it or its cause. He rode abaft her mewsany on purpose, and kept a watchful look out to the rear. The peril sprouted from the front, suddenly, in a long line of riders breasting a hill and racing down with wild war whoops upon them.

Their own mounts were tired and dispirited. With two riders up, they could never outrun this cavalry that pounded down now, glittering in the first light of the suns. Armor winked in ruby and jade fire. Lanceheads glittered. Feathers waved. Dust spurted back in a long line. The riders bore on and opened out into a circle, ringing the fugitives.

Seg slid his bow forward and nocked his single shaft.

They'd done well and come a long way—and now they'd come to the end of their flight.

He looked into the faces of these warriors.

Skull faces . . . Blunt-featured, with a tightly drawn skin of pebbly gray-green, with the roots of the teeth exposed, with bony brow ridges overhanging smoky crimson eyes, these faces looked the decomposing features of nightmare newly risen from the grave. Bamba let out a shriek of horror. Malindi fainted clean away. The ghastly riders ringed their quarry.

Milsi urged her mount a little forward. She held up her hand.

"Lahal and Lahal! Well met!"

"Lahal, majestrix!" said the leader, his gruesome features writhing with an emotion that might indicate pleasure. "Thank the Good Pandrite we have found you safe at last!"

# CHAPTER EIGHTEEN
## The queen calls: "Hai, Jikai!"

"I," said Skort the Clawsang, "was told you were dead, majestrix, in that confounded Coup Blag." He used the teeth that appeared to be decomposing to bite firmly into a slice of succulent roast vosk. They were sitting around the camp fire and they were eating and drinking until they burst.

"It was poor Milsi who died. She had the same name as me, as you know, and I grieve for her."

"Aye." Skort wiped his lipless mouth, daintily. "But, majestrix, it is not all good news. That foul cramph Muryan has not released your daughter, the divine Princess Mishti—"

"What!" The regal anger that blazed from Milsi made Seg realize that, by Vox, she was a queen.

"He would not release her into our care, as was ordered. We rode to seek a ruling on this, and our spies told us of the Warvol Tower. But—" and Skort added this very rapidly. "—he would not harm her. He dare not."

"That I believe to be true. But I'll—I'll—"

"Do what all queens do, particularly Queens of Pain, and have his head off," said Seg, and buried his face in a tankard of parclear.

"Oh, I shall, I shall! Disabuse yourself of any notion that I will not, Seg the Horkandur!"

Skort, with a mastery of tactics that pleased Seg, chipped in to say: "I own I am surprised to find you here, Seg, and yet pleased. Very pleased. The queen has need of all the champions who will muster to her banner."

"There's going to be a fight, then?"

"Assuredly, a fight, and a battle."

"What of Kov Llipton?"

"If only," said Milsi, "I could trust him!"

Carefully, Skort said: "Your husband, King Crox, suffered the misfortune of having his wife and family killed in an accident. Luckily for us, that brought you here, majestrix, an event for which we are profoundly grateful. This rast Muryan callously slew his wife and family just so that he might marry you, according to the laws. Kov Llipton still has a wife and family. Also, he is a numim."

"I heard Muryan's family fell under a Rapa's garbage cart," said Seg.

"Under a garbage cart, yes. They did not fall. They were pushed."

"And I'll bet that Strom Ornol did the pushing."

"Just so." Skort swiveled that macabre head and his crimson eyes rested balefully upon the queen. "Llipton may be a numim. But there is nothing in the law that says he may not marry an apim. The marriage would be in name only. But then he would be king."

"You think that is his design, Skort?" Milsi looked completely undecided. "You know the

River, Skort, you understand local conditions. I am from Jholaix, and . . ."

"My own personal belief is that Llipton is upright and honest in his own way. He took much upon himself when the king your husband gave him the charge of the kingdom. He may be overstrict. But I believe him to be loyal."

"Yeah," said Seg. "But to whom?"

"To King Crox until the king is known to be dead."

"And then to the queen?"

"That is what I believe."

"One thing is certain, Llipton won't have Muryan as a king set above him."

"Ha!"

"If there is to be a battle," and here Milsi spoke with a wistful regret, "Muryan is able to field a formidable force, as he told me with much relish."

"We'll gulp him down with relish!"

"Yes, good Skort, I pray the Almighty Pandrite this will be so. But there was a man in the guard set over us, a man with red hair. A famous archer. He boasted continually of his prowess and of that of his men."

"Oh?" said Seg, at once alert, his professional hackles raised. "His name?"

"He was a Jiktar, commanding a regiment. His name was Nag-So-Spangchin, called Spangchin the Horkandur."

"A whole regiment!"

"Aye, Seg—and his name, like yours—he wore the golden zhantil-head of the pakzhan at his throat and was a zhanpaktun, although he insisted on being addressed as a hyrpaktun, which he said was proper—"

Seg put out his hand and touched Milsi's hand, feeling the tremble. She stilled instantly the moment he touched her.

Following her line, he said: "This is the coming fashion, to call hyrpaktuns zhanpaktuns, to dub paktuns mortpaktuns, and to let the ordinary mercenaries wallow in the name of paktuns. But a whole regiment! This is bad news indeed."

"Aye." Skort nodded his horrific corpselike head. "All men know of the fame of the Bowmen of Loh."

"He wore a flaunting mass of red and yellow feathers in his helmet, and, Seg, his bow was very like yours."

"And his arrows were all fletched blue with the feathers of the king korf from my own mountains of Erthyrdrin!"

"Yes, Seg . . ."

There was no need to enlarge. Pandahem, like many another island and country, had once been under the heel of the Empire of Walfarg, that was known as the Empire of Loh. The Gold and Red banners had waved in those days, until the empire had fallen and the continent of Loh had turned inward upon itself, mysterious behind its walled gardens, its women wearing veils, soft-slippered and soft-spoken. Now the new countries of Pandahem and the Empire of Vallia were pressing outwards. But men remembered the merciless efficiency of the armies of Walfarg, where every other man had red hair, and of the sleeting death brought to every battlefield by the Bowmen of Loh.

Out of his own jumbled thoughts Seg said

fretfully: "I wish we could find Obolya so that I might have my own longbow again."

No one had heard of the whereabouts of Obolya, and it was assumed he was busily trading for saddle animals.

The queen stood up. Everyone else scrambled to their feet. Looking at her, Seg felt the blood in him, the bursting pressure of his heart beating. She lifted her chin.

"We will not be downhearted, my friends! We will go forward, confident in Pandrite. If there is to be a battle then we shall win it. And then we shall make a just administration of all the land. Hai, jikai!"

"Hai, jikai!" they roared, caught up in the abrupt splendor of the moment. Seg yelled, too . . .

Considering it markedly inadvisable to go anywhere near Mewsansmot where Trylon Muryan hatched his plans, they skirted the town out on the plains before rejoining the river line much farther downstream. Worry over her daughter made Milsi pale and fretful; yet Seg marked the way she contained her irritability and temper with the Clawsangs. Despite continual reassurances that Muryan would not dare to harm the lady Mishti, she took scant comfort, and lived on only by virtue of her own courage and inner resources. Seg watched all this.

No word of love passed between them. His own tangled emotions had still not fully recovered, and Milsi had more than enough problems to contend with. He took every opportunity to reassure her, and she responded in a way that while not listless, saddened him. She spoke bravely, and she encouraged all; but inwardly, Seg sensed, she doubted a happy outcome to this business.

At the capital, Nalvinlad, two items of news greeted them, one good, one evil.

The good news came when Bamba, screaming, flew into the arms of Diomb. The dinkus hugged each other with a frank and open display of affection that made Seg heave up a sigh, and then castigate himself for a dreaming loon. Milsi put a scrap of yellow lace to her eye. In the next instant, there outside her palace of the Langal Paraido, Khardun, the Dorvenhork, Rafikhan, Naghan the Slippy, Caphlander and Umtig with Lord Clinglin waving his eight arms on his breast, gathered around, shouting the Lahals. Hundle the Design had been pardoned and had gone off home. So the reunion was splendid.

The bad news was that Kov Llipton and six of his chief men had been treacherously attacked. Only Llipton and Trylon Ronglor had survived, badly wounded. It was thought that Llipton might recover, given time and the devoted attentions of the needlemen.

Vad Olmengo brought this news to the queen. This was the real Olmengo, and with his chin beard and full face he did not look much like Strom Ornol; but that disguise had proved perfectly adequate again.

"The rast impersonated me and brought his assassins into the palace, majestrix! The guards slew many of these vile stikitches; but the poor Kov was struck through. I am desolate—"

"It is a sad business, Olmengo, but the kov will survive, as we trust in the good Pandrite."

"I pray so, my queen." Here Olmengo's face drew down mournfully. "But the soldiers! The generals had chosen that night to confer, and the

Kapts are slain. We have no one with experience of warfare to lead the army!''

Seg kept very quiet. He did not want to be landed with that job. Oh, no, by Vox, not him!

Milsi said, sharply: ''Then the senior Chuktars will decide. Muryan will attack. There is no doubt of that!''

In a very quiet voice as they all trooped up into the palace, Seg said to the Krozair: ''Look, Pur Zarado. I know of the fame of the Krozairs. You are great warriors. If these folk have no generals, surely you could—''

''Your pardon, Seg. I am a Krozair of Zamu, as my comrade Zunder was a Krozair of Zimuzz. We are hard fighting men, yes; we do not aspire to the rarefied heights of being a Kapt, not even a Chuktar. I imagine I could swagger well enough as a Jiktar and bully a regiment. But . . . Oh, no!''

A couple of days later Skort's spies reported that Muryan's army was moving south.

Seg quite expected a huge flotilla of schinkitrees to sail down river. Skort scoffed at this.

''What! No, my friend, no sensible man wages a war on the river. Victor as well as vanquished is likely to fall into the water. Then, well. . . .''

''Yes, I see.''

''We will march out and the battle will take place where the forest gives way to a nice battle-worthy terrain.''

''Who is to command?''

''The Chuktars argue among themselves. Men are coming in well enough to fill the ranks. Kov Llipton may not be King Crox, may Clansawft of the Perimeters have him in his keeping. But the kov is now recognized as being a man with honor attempting to carry out the duties entrusted to him. He maintained the law.''

''Oh, aye, he did that.''

''And men see that Muryan is a villain. His own adherents ride in fear of him, believe me. I have high hopes for the outcome of the battle.''

''Without a leader on our side.''

''The queen will decide.''

''Well, she'd best decide damned soon.''

Skort swished his sword back, and looked sharply at Seg. Then he said: ''The sorest point at issue is this matter of the queen's daughter. We know where she is held. But it would take an army to break through—and that is what our army will do under the queen's direction.''

''Oh?'' Seg's mouth did not drop open. ''You mean Milsi will handle the battle herself?''

''No, no, Seg, you great fambly! That is the aim of the battle, to smash Muryan and to break through to the lady Mishti and rescue her.''

Seg rubbed a hand down a raspy jaw. ''It's these Bowmen of Loh who worry me.'' Incautiously he went on: ''If I commanded them they'd win the battle on their own.''

''But, horter Seg, you command nothing. And you and your comrades live in the palace at the generous hands of the queen.''

He felt like saying snappishly: ''She owes us that!''

The next time Seg was talking to Zarado, the Krozair caught him up in an excited torrent of words.

''When I was fighting in Vallia for Jak the Drang he often used to say, very many times: 'If

only Seg were here!' I wonder, Seg Segutorio the
Horkandur—''

"Oh, there are many Segs in the world.''

"That may be true; but I have been puzzled
where I had heard the name before.''

"They still have not chosen a Kapt to lead
them. Surely, Pur Zarado—''

"By Zim-Zair! As Zogo the Hyr-Whip is my
judge! Not me!''

That evening Seg was just preparing to turn in
in the room allotted to him high in the Chungi
Tower. Milsi entered without knocking. She looked
splendid. Her hair was coiffed and sheened with
health, her cheeks glowed, her eyes—well, Seg
could lose everything in those eyes of hers. She
wore a pale blue gown, loose and flowing, girded
by a thin golden chain from which hung a jeweled
dagger. Seg swallowed.

"Majestrix—''

"The intelligence is that Muryan will reach the
spot chosen for the battle in two days. You, Seg
Segutorio the Horkandur, will lead my army in the
fight.''

"But—''

"Do you truly love me?''

"Yes.''

"Then that is settled.'' And she stepped forward
into the clasp of his Bowman's arms.

# CHAPTER NINETEEN

## The Battle of the Kazzchun River

At the queen's express command Kapt Seg wore a bronze harness garnished with golden rosettes. His bronze helmet fitted close, and the blue and white and yellow feathers flew high above on their golden spike. His tunic was of red velvet, lustrous and cunningly changing in hue and tone with the angle of the lights. He strapped on his own drexer, and a plethora of other weapons also. He looked a fitting figure to command an army.

At Kapt Seg's express wish and desire the queen wore a bronze harness, garnished with golden rosettes. Her helmet with its feathers framed her face glowing with passion and conviction in the right and in victory. She wore the Kregan arsenal of weaponry, and Seg's heart joyed in her.

Above them lofted the flag the queen had commanded to be made and embroidered specially for Seg. This was his own tresh. Tall and narrow, it was of red silk. In careful fine stitching in golden thread her handmaidens had represented a bow in the lower portion, bent to shoot upward. Instead of an arrow, a jagged bolt of lightning, lethal and overpowering, skewered skyward.

"Do you then expect me to challenge the heavens themselves?"

"If any man dared—"

Seg looked at her. He could see only Milsi, sitting erect and supple in the saddle, see her gorgeousness. He smiled. He had no need to prattle on about daring anything for her. By the Veiled Froyvil! She knew that!

The army marched out.

Vad Olmengo, quivering, had exuded an enormous sigh of satisfaction and relief when the queen told him that Kapt Seg would take command. Had the chief place been thrust upon him . . . !

Seg had a plan.

"It is not a great plan, Milsi, not a mind-shattering exhibition of military genius. But a plan we must have."

"I believe in you, Seg, as you know. Therefore your plan is good."

"Ridiculous!"

On the day before the battle Skort had taken Seg out to survey the field of the forthcoming conflict. They fought to protocol here along the Kazzchun River. He recalled the fracas between the dinkus, and he half-smiled. These armored and mounted warriors with their bronze and leather armor and their steel weapons had not progressed very far along the path of military skills. . . .

He gave the Chulik, Nath Chandarl the Dorvenhork, his instructions. The Chulik nodded, cunning in the ways of battle.

"It shall be as you say, Seg the Horkandur.

There may not be many of us, but I will make
them fight like demons from the Pits of Gundarlo!''

"And," put in the Khibil, Khardun the Franch,
"my lads will hit them with such élan they will all
turn tail and run."

"Make it so, and may Likshu the Treacherous
and Horato the Potent look down with benediction
upon you."

When he spoke to the Rapa, Rafikhan, Seg
called down the benediction of Rhapaporgolam the
Reiver of Souls.

"I have my task, set to my hands, Seg. It shall
be done."

The Jiktars and the three Chuktars of the little
army did not demur when Kapt Seg set his own
men thus in positions of vital importance. Seg
spoke to them. They saw they were dealing with a
man who commanded, who had commanded, who
knew how to command. They saw his strength, of
will and determination as well as of body. He had
much of the yrium, that mystical aura of power,
charisma, that made men and women follow him
willy-nilly. Seg himself made no pretense to the
yrium. He was not aware of the charismatic presence he conveyed when he wanted something
done . . .

Two of the Chuktars commanded each his wing
of the infantry. This was chiefly composed of
half-naked men, many of them fishermen with
bundles of their long and cruelly-barbed fishspears.
These they would hurl with deadly accuracy. Long
before they came within range the Bowmen of Loh
would have destroyed them. The infantry carried
shields, large, pointed at top and bottom, fashioned of withies or wood, a few with leather, and

if there was one in fifty with a bronze rim that was overstating the case.

The remaining Chuktar commanded the cavalry, mewsany-mounted men who were a trifle better armored than the infantry. They carried lances, small shields, and some had javelins. Each regiment was separated out as to type under its Jiktar, and, perforce, owing to training, Seg had to continue with this arrangement.

Skort, well armed and armored, rode close with his Clawsangs. He said: "I now believe this Jiktar Nag-So-Spangchin, known as the Horkandur, commands a regiment of three hundred to three hundred and fifty Bowmen of Loh."

"A formidable force." Seg knew damn well how truly formidable a force that was. "The Dorvenhork will play his part, Skort. Chuliks detest being beaten."

"Who does not?"

"True. But there is something in a soulless Chulik that cannot abide defeat. And I do not believe the Dorvenhork to be soulless, contrary to received opinion."

"There are few who would agree with you."

"There must be Chuliks and Chuliks, as there are apims and apims, and, doubtless, Clawsangs and Clawsangs."

"Aye. But not Katakis and Katakis."

"How many?"

Skort could not pull his lip, but his lipless mouth gleamed blue. "We believe no more than two hundred and fifty."

"Then they must be put down."

"Oh, aye."

Caphlander the Relt rode up on a zorca. Seg

gaped at him. He wore a leather jerkin, belted in very tightly, very tightly indeed. His feathered head was covered by a leather cap, in which flourished further feathers—clearly these were not his own. He gave a hesitant salute.

"Well, Caphlander. What does this mean?"

"Why, Seg the Horkandur, merely that I may not fight, but I am a trained stylor. I can carry messages."

The queen smiled graciously. "You are right welcome, master Caphlander. If every man and woman play their parts as well as you, then victory will smile upon our banners this day."

As to that, grumped Seg to himself, there were altogether too many damned banners and flags and standards. If each one prevented its bearer from striking a blow he'd see the lot consigned to Cottmer's Caverns.

He glanced up at the standard Milsi had given him. It really was rather splendid. Its bearer, a horrific-looking Clawsang called Tskarin, would have to be carefully watched, for if that banner fell the warriors and the men who had come to swell the ranks might very well run off.

His trumpeter, another corpselike Clawsang called Ksandic, had proved he knew the calls regulations laid down in the army of Croxdrin—trouble was, did all the people in the ranks know them as well?

Diomb had gone off with the Dorvenhork, beside himself with glee that he was seeing more of the outside world—this time how they got on when they had a real big fight. Seg had had to let him go. Bamba had not cried; in fact Bamba was not about when Diomb marched off. Clearly—Seg knew about and understood these things—quite clearly

Bamba had equipped herself and had skulked off to join Diomb. Oh, well. . . . As for Malindi, she had wailed when Milsi rode off; but a single stern injunction had stilled the pretty infantlike features. A battlefield was no place for a Syblie—well, to be truthful, it was no place at all for anyone with a scrap of sense in their heads.

Military organization must, of course, vary over the wide world of Kregen; in these parts the old methods of the defunct Empire of Walfarg persisted. Usually there were ten men in an audo, eight or ten audos in a pastang, and six pastangs to a regiment. Milsi's army as Seg watched them marching out to war were on the low side in regimental strengths. The men raised by King Crox into regular regiments and with whom he had carved out his kingdom, were well enough armed and equipped and trained. Their regiments usually totalled around the four hundred mark. The half-naked fisherfolk and townsmen and riff-raff from the streets, although prettily organized, could muster few regiments above the three hundred and fifty or sixty mark.

This would have to suffice. It was pretty certain that the regiments marching under Trylon Muryan's brown and white banners would muster roughly equal numbers to those with the queen. It was those confounded Bowmen of Loh. . . .

The moment the priests from the various temples had ceased their chantings and incantations and the sacrifices had been made, Seg breathed more freely. The bands started up, blowing and banging lustily. A little breeze got up and blew the banners bravely. The army presented a fine sight, swinging along with the bands playing and the standards flying, and the men singing. Seg humped along on his zorca and tried not to feel too angry at the waste of it all.

The bands played "The Jaws that Bite, the Teeth that Rend." Then they went into "The Forest Stands from Dawn to Dusk." With a fine flush of fury, Seg supposed that cramph Muryan would have his bands playing "The Bowman of Loh."

His mind obsessed with the plan for the battle oddly enough rejected further worry. He found himself thinking of what Milsi had told him of her childhood. Her mother had been born in Jholaix, daughter of one of the wealthy Wine Families. Her grandmother had been born in Nalvindrin, second daughter of the king and queen of the time. Uprisings and revolutions had found, in the end, her grand aunt married and the queen—and her daughter had brought King Crox to the throne—and her grandmother safely hidden in Jholaix. But descent came down through the female line, and Milsi was the one and only legitimate Queen Mab. Thus had all the problems arisen.

All the girls of the family were called Mab as well as their given name. If Milsi happened to be slain, either in this battle or at the hands of Muryan's hired assassins led by Strom Ornol, then the lady Mishti Mab would inherit the legal descent. No doubt that was what Muryan, having lost Milsi, now planned. The thought that if it came to it Seg would slay the cramph Muryan without mercy gave him no comfort whatsoever.

The idea that he had engineered the deaths of the Bowmen of Loh—or would have done if his primitive plan succeeded—gave him so much less comfort as to make him feel that he bore the sins of the world upon his shoulders. Oh, they weren't his own countrymen. They had red hair, therefore they came from Walfarg. His land of Erthyrdrin, in the northernmost tip of Loh, had been ravaged and attacked by Walfarg over the centuries. Erthyrdrin provided the very cream of the Bowmen of Loh. All the same, it went sore to him to do this thing, and he just wanted this stupid battle over and out of the way so that the future could be entered into sooner rather than later—or at all. . . .

The army reached the area selected for the fight.

To the right flank stretched the river, masked off by a screen of closely growing vegetation. The ground lay open, dotted with a few trees, scattered outposts of the forest, and most of the left flank was open and rolling, ideal country for cavalry maneuver.

As this was what amounted to a north–south confrontation along the Kazzchun River the northern forces must have a marked preponderance of cavalry. They were the people who tended the vast herds of mewsanys and provided them to the southerners, after all. Chuktar Ortyg Lloton na Mismot, who was a trylon, commanding Milsi's cavalry, had a stern task ahead. He had most of the nobility riding in his ranks.

With all the cavalry available to the enemy, Seg calculated that Muryan would attempt to work the old door hinge ploy on him. He'd use some of his cavalry to shoulder the mewsany riders of Milsi's army aside, and then just ride around from his right flank, using his anchored left infantry as the hinge, and roll Seg and all his people up and crush them against the river. If they all went swimming,

well, that would put a little extra zest in Trylon
Muryan's day.

Inquiries of his infantry commanders elicited the
information that soldiers always fought by regiment,
and the regiments in their higher groupings always
fought together, as was proper.

Chuktar Moldo Nirgra na Chefensmot, who was
a strom, wrinkled up his forehead when Seg gave
him his orders.

"We need to hold, Chuktar Moldo. This you
will do."

"My regulars will stand, Kapt Seg. We are
skilled with the strangchi. But—the scum you foist
on me—"

"Not scum, Chuktar! Men like you or me. They
may be fishermen or laborers but they can fight.
You will need the fishspears, believe me." Then
Seg went more deeply into just what these ill-
disciplined bands of half-naked men throwing cruelly barbed spears might do when allied with the
solid ranks of the regulars.

The strangchi, long-hafted, topped by spear-point,
axe-head and hook, was not the strangdja of Chem,
that holly-leafed lethality; in these circumstances it
ought to prove superior. If it failed, Seg's army
would go splashing into the brown waters.

Chuktar Moldo loosed the collar of his tunic
under the rim of his corselet, the kax gilded and
brave with engravings of stirring battle scenes.

"It is these Bowmen of Loh, Kapt, that—"

Seg lowered a baleful glance on the infantry
commander. "I have seen mercenaries refuse their
hire and run when they heard they were to face
Bowmen of Loh. But you are not mercenaries.
You fight for your queen! And our mercenary

archers are Undurkers, who have a great contempt for Bowmen of Loh.''

With that Seg finished off his instructions, and he thought with his own professional arrogance that he'd always considered these condescending Undurkers a bunch of idiots. Still, they would have to serve this day. . . .

Mixing his light troops, his kreutzin, with his regulars in the right wing, under Chuktar Nath Roynlair na Strainsmot, who also was a strom, he gave similar orders. The difference here was that, Chuktar Nath being a numim, he said: ''And on the signal you will charge and let nothing stand in your way. Is that clear?''

''As the streets clear when the rains come, Kapt Seg.''

Trust a lion-man for that way of expressing it!

Milsi looked radiant when Seg trotted across to her. The army moved out ahead, deploying to orders. The suns streamed their mingled brilliance upon the field. Away ahead the long serried masses of the enemy came into view, dark and ominous. Seg began checking off numbers, and Milsi watched him, her face expressing as it were in reflection every nuance of Seg's as he counted and calculated.

''Well,'' he said, and turned to Milsi. ''He has more cavalry, as we expected. But he is deficient in infantry. And that is mostly mercenary, and some rascally low-class masichieri among 'em, I'll warrant, no better than brigands.''

''He does not really need footsoldiers, does he? He simply puts his Bowmen of Loh to the fore, they shoot and shoot and we are pinned, and his cavalry ride around and—oh, Seg! What have we done!''

"You simply have a slight case of the twitches before battle, nothing to worry about. Everybody has 'em."

"Seg!"

"D'you see, Milsi? We are not deploying out to our left. See? All his gorgeous and famous cavalry are facing empty ground."

"Yes, but—"

"Now watch!"

Trumpets, pealing high and shrill into the clear air, banners, floating and fluttering over the hosts, the dull surf-roar of hundreds of men, the clink and clash of iron and bronze, the excited shrilling of mewsanys and the harsh breath of dust clogging mouths and nostrils. . . .

"They move!"

The Bowmen of Loh trotted out ahead, smart, their bows curves of glitter in the light. By reason of Seg's clumped formations close to his right flank, the archers perforce had to move to their left flank. "They must be licking their lips over there to see such massed targets," said Seg. He looked to the screen of trees following the line of the river.

Out from that concealment ran men, archers, haughty canine faces slanted sideways as they raised their composite bows. Leading them roared on the Dorvenhork. They flanked the Bowmen of Loh. They were well within their shorter range. They began to play on the famed Bowmen of Loh, shooting with flat trajectories that worked down the line like a meat slicer.

Seg smiled. "Very nice. I sent them there in boats before dawn. And, see! There goes Khardun with our paktuns! Oh, he has them by the short and curlies! And Rafikhan!''

Left out on a limb, the cavalry commanded by Muryan started to charge into the left flank of Milsi's army. And, of course, they were met by a hedge of steel and by a multitude of showered fishspears that discomposed them mightily. When Chuktar Ortyg brought Seg's cavalry into action they charged slap bang into the flank of the enemy jutmen and knocked them over, sent them reeling, all jammed up in a tightly wedged mass of frightened and ungovernable animals and men.

Chuktar Nath Roynlair, being a numim, wasn't going to delay when a fight was promised and he simply led his people in a blood-crazed charge dead ahead. This finished Muryan's left wing. His right wing was in process of taking itself off as fast as the mewsanys could gallop. That left the center. Here Chuktar Moldo, having held the charge of hostile jutmen, having seen them repulsed and routed, was feeling mightily puffed up. His trumpeter blew ''Charge!'' and it was all over.

''Very satisfactory,'' said Seg Segutorio. ''By the Veiled Froyvil, yes!''

''Seg!'' said Milsi, staring at him as though she could never bear to tear her gaze away. ''My Jikai!''

# CHAPTER TWENTY

## Seg casts a reasonable shaft

"Now let us get after the rast!"

As they spurred ahead, Seg reflected that Milsi was a romantic soul. Well, she had every right to be, seeing what her life had been and what she had been through. Her feelings and expression left him in no doubt. When she dubbed him her Jikai—she meant it with a full heart.

With Skort and his Clawsangs riding in attendance and with Seg's comrades joining with a few of the Undurker archers, they caught up with the fleeing Muryan in not too long a time. He had a small party of adherents still with him, including the red-headed Bowman of Loh, Nag-So-Spangchin.

The configuration of the ground here, a series of shallow depressions and low rounded hills, channelled pursued and pursuers into the valley to the right ahead, which looked broader and easier than the left. The flight hullaballooed along, with the dust kicking and the mewsanys stretching their necks, clumsily thumping on in their six-legged gait.

At the far end of the valley the ground leveled off and stretched off to the next horizon. A clump of trees to the left showed up clearly, with an overturned carriage nearby.

Muryan's party halted.

Seg saw men gesticulating up there and arms raised in anger. Just to the left an uncrossable ravine split the ground. Instantly, Seg saw it all.

So did Milsi.

"Mishti!" she screamed, rising in her stirrups, staring wildly at the small white form trapped beneath one of the shafts of the overturned carriage. A tiny arm waved.

The Dorvenhork in his Chulik way growled to his archers; "Shaft 'em all!"

The canine-faced archers loosed, uselessly. Seg's hand reached around for his apology for a longbow. He had but the one arrow, which he had brought out of comfort, for, as he was the first to say, he felt naked without a good Lohvian longbow and a quiver of clothyard shafts.

Milsi urged her mount toward the ravine; but the beast, sensible in his mewsany way, refused to descend.

Abruptly, the paktuns about Muryan leveled their lances, helmets came down, and they charged pell-mell upon Milsi's party. Skort bellowed and leveled his lance.

Milsi saw what followed. Everyone saw. Nag-so-Spangchin jumped off his mount. He stood proud from the few men still with Muryan. He lifted his bow. The arrow head glittered sharply in the lights of Zim and Genodras. He loosed.

The shaft spat from the bow, soaring up and up. No trained eye was needed to tell where that steel-tipped bird would fall.

"Mishti!" screamed Milsi, frantic, panting, wild-eyed.

Useless to shaft the Bowman of Loh. Too late for that. The charging cavalry with their leveled lances were almost on Seg's people, who rode out to front that wild and desperate last onslaught.

The bow was in Seg's hand. The bow he had knocked up with a knife, working hurriedly, an unseasoned bow, which he had shot in once, a poor apology for a bow, and yet the only bow here that was of any use whatsoever. The silly leaf-fletched shaft was nocked in a twinkling. He could feel the blood, he could feel his heart, he could feel his muscles. He stopped breathing. He laid himself into his bow, holding him just so, every single fiber of his being wrapped up in the shot. Left and right hands drawing together, right hand to the ear and left arm thrusting out with sure power and purpose. The loose, clean, clean! The shaft, speeding away, like a hunting bird, like a gleaming raptor of the skies swooping upon some poor fluttering prey.

High and high against the blue soared the shaft.

It curved. It dipped. Unheard through the thundering oncoming racket of the deadly cavalry charge, arrow struck arrow.

Both shafts tumbled to the ground.

And a damned great mewsany lumbered full into Seg and knocked him all sprawling, and a razor-edged lance point sliced all along his side. The animal fell on him, a bulky sweaty body clad in bronze fell on him and all the lights went out for

Seg and he was gathered up into the all-enveloping cloak of Notor Zan.

When he regained his senses the famous Bells of Beng Kishi so rang and clamored in his head that he dare not so much as move that poor abused cranium of his.

They carted him back to Nalvinlad, first in a creaking two-wheeled conveyance drawn by a couple of mytzers and then in a schinkitree. His head still jumped about loosely upon his shoulders. They put him in a fine expensive bed in a splendid bedroom and the doctors with their needles stuck him and took away the pain, and so he slept.

Milsi kept watch and ward over him. He came to, at last, for Seg had bathed in the Sacred Pool of Baptism in the River Zelph in far Aphrasöe, the Swinging City. He supposed, logically, that he would take Milsi to Aphrasöe very soon. Then she too, besides partaking of this miraculous recovery from injuries, would also live a thousand years.

"Muryan?" he said when Milsi came in, smiling.

"Oh, don't worry your head about him. He never was a good swimmer."

"The lady Mishti?"

Milsi frowned.

"I own I do not understand her. She is still a child yet she is grown into womanhood—and, yet, Seg, she sometimes acts as though she were my mother. It is strange."

"That's children for you."

"You must mend soon. We are being married in six days."

"If you say so, my heart. If you are sure."

"I am certain positive! Do you not wish to be king?"

Seg did not answer but picked a paline from the
gold dish at the bedside and chewed comfortably.
Truth to tell, he didn't know about this kingship
business. He'd been a kov, and kind-heartedness
had got him nowhere. Perhaps being a king where
they sent people off for a little swim might also
prove untenable as a way of life.

"My love!" she cried, and plumped down on
the bed and took him in her arms. "I want for you
only what is best!"

"I want to marry you, Milsi. You know my
past. I own I feel for you so much that—well—"

"We were both shafted by the same bolt of
lightning." She laughed, joyful at her own clever-
ness. "That is the lightning bolt upon your flag,
Seg, my dearest heart!"

Holding her close, drawing in the sweet per-
fume of her hair and shoulders, feeling her firm
softness against him, Seg fell into a dizzy state of
contentment that overpowered him with its fresh-
ness and delight. That this could be! He gave
thanks to all the gods and spirits of Kregen that he
should be so favored, so fortunate, so blessed.

Preparations for the wedding went ahead and a
couple of days later the lady Mishti slipped in to
see him.

She surprised Seg. Milsi had been quite right.
This slip of a girl, half woman, half child, knew
exactly what she wanted, and was unsure only of
the best way to gain her ends. She did not look at
all like Milsi, and her hair was dark, her nose thin,
and her mouth rather too full. Still, she would
grow out of imperfections and become a dazzling
beauty.

She said: "Kov Llipton mends, pantor Seg. You are to be my new father. Well, mother is old. One day I shall be queen, and very soon, I think. Then, I am almost decided, I shall marry Kov Llipton. He is a numim, of course; but then he will die and I shall marry whomever I choose and have a great deal of money—lots and lots. . . ."

"Go," said Seg, "away. Come back when you can talk respectfully of your mother. Is that clear!"

She jumped into the air, her face blanched, she bit her lip—turned and fled.

Seg started to berate himself, cursing his own folly and pig-headed stupidity. Onker! Vosk-skulled onker!

Now he'd ruptured the whole fabric of his planned life.

Nothing of what had passed was spoken, the days went by, and, suddenly, here he was being dressed in robes so ornate as to need another fellow in here with him to help support the weight. He made sure he had his drexer with him. Obolya had been through on his way downriver, taking Seg's bowstave and quiver with him. Oh, well. He could look forward with pleasure at least to building himself a new bow on his honeymoon. . . . He fretted over Mishti. . . .

The wedding took place in the Temple of Pandrite Risen, and included priests of all the other temples of the city. The occasion was in truth splendid. So much gold, so much glitter, so many lamps, so many robes of wonderful ornateness. The music soared. The scents almost overpowered. The choirs sang. The lady Mishti stood to the side, drenched in silks and gold, and her eyes were downcast and she did not look at her new father at all.

One could feel true sorrow and sympathy for any girl who has to face a new father; that does not mean she may forfeit her respect for her mother. Seg felt his heart move for poor Mishti. He would do all he could, and perhaps that would not be enough.

When the dancing began he said to Milsi: "This is a splendid wedding, my heart. But there must be at least two more you know."

"Oh, aye, assuredly. One with all my friends in Jholaix. And the other with yours in Vallia."

"The Vallia of today is not like the Vallia you were taught to hate as a child."

"I know. I have spoken to Llipton on this."

He was there, the kov, propped up, joying in the happiness of his queen. His wife, the gorgeous Rahishta, was truly sumptuous and Seg couldn't see Llipton having her killed off.

They were enjoying themselves in the enormous ballroom of the Langarl Paraido. Perfumes scented the air, fans waved, wine circulated, people talked and chattered and danced as the four orchestras played by turn. Seg, looking at Milsi, found he could hardly bear to look away. She so radiated happiness, she looked so perfect, that she dominated everything by her own self and not because she happened to be the queen.

On the second day of the ceremonies, Seg was to be crowned king.

This function took place in the throne room of the Langal Paraido. More gorgeousness, more gold, more silks and tapestries, more of everything luxurious and sybaritic and heady with the promise of the life to come.

Clad in robes of astounding magnificence, Seg

stood forth with Milsi facing him. She was the only person with the power to crown him. She wore a long straight gown of purest white, girded in silver, with the crown upon her head. The chief priest held upon a velvet cushion the crown she would take up and place upon Seg's dark unruly mop.

He stared up into her eyes. So beautiful, so wonderful—a girl who was his wife now. Yet, yet—did he want to be king of this infernal jungly rivery place?

Milsi took up the crown. She held it high and all sound ceased in that immense chamber. The chief priest stood like a dummy. A priest beside him stood on one leg, the other stilled in the act of scratching his calf. The feathered fans ceased their incessant waving to and fro. A little fly upon the velvet cushion stopped and did not move.

Seg knew.

He turned his head and looked at the water clock fixed beneath the east window. No water dropped from the clepsydra's upper chamber. The water in the lower stood as though solid, like a sheet of blued steel.

The blue water in the upper chamber remained where it was, fixed, rigid, solid, unmoving. . . .

Motionless in their ranks all his comrades stood looking blindly on. All the nobles and the chiefs, all the great ones, all the vast assembly—all—stood like stone.

In all that great and glittering company only two lives sparked with energy. Milsi lowered the crown, and almost dropped it, and so placed it back upon the velvet cushion.

"Seg! What is it? What—?"

"It is all right, Milsi, I promise you—"

"But—but—" She looked around, distraught.

He took the two steps up and clasped her in his arms, smoothing the supple curve of her back for he could not smooth her hair for the crown.

"Milsi, hush, hush—"

A golden yellow light blossomed about them. The unearthly scent of surpassing sweetness enfolded them. At the core of the golden radiance the figure of a woman glowed, supernal, divine, shedding benediction. She wore a white gown girdled by a golden chain. Her dark hair flowed in a loose perfumed mass from beneath a helmet of so brilliant a gold it shone as though molten. Crimson plumes bedecked the helmet. Milsi, looking on in awe, saw the woman's face.

A pale face, unlined, with a purity of outline that set her countenance apart from ordinary features, her face half-smiled down upon the two locked in each other's arms. Her eyes of a deep and lustrous brown seemed to melt into them. Her firm, full mouth, a contrast of complexity, curved benignly upon them. Yet in her left hand she held a sword. Upon her breast shone an insignia in the shape of a wheel with nine projections upon its outer circumference.

Seg felt Milsi stir in his arms, stiffen, grow firm.

"Who," demanded Milsi, "are you, lady?"

The answering voice flowed in a golden mellow sound like a million deep and yet happy-toned bells all chiming from the bell towers of a world's temples.

"I speak to the Grand Archbold of the Kroveres of Iztar."

"I am here, my lady Zena Iztar," said Seg. "And I give you Lahal and Lahal, and my devotion, and ask you to share with me my happiness and pride in my lady, the lady Milsi, who is the queen of this land."

"Bravely spoken, Seg Segutorio. But you forget you are my Grand Archbold. To you has been entrusted the futherance of my Order."

"I own to a parlous state of sin in this, for I have been neglectful of late. Yet there have been reasons—"

"Reasons enough so that I have not called on you beforetime. But, now, you are not fighting the Shanks. You are not battling the adherents of Lem the Silver Leem. You are not putting down the slavers, the aragorn, the slavemasters. You are not opposing the Werefolk. You are not combatting the Traxon Ardueres. And you do nothing about the Witch of Loh, Csitra, who commands Spikatur Hunting Sword."

"That is true. I *am* being married."

Milsi could feel the hardness of Seg against her. Her common sense told her that this apparition was real, a visitation from the gods—perhaps a goddess herself. So that her Seg took much upon himself to answer in so proud a fashion.

Zena Iztar's smile curved more. "I joy in your good fortune in the lady Milsi, Seg. But do you wish to stay here as king?"

"I do not know! I wish to stay with Milsi—that is all I do know. And, my lady, I wish to serve you as best I may."

"Do you forget what the Emperor of Vallia drew out for your future possibilities, Seg? Concerning Pandahem?"

"I do not forget. He suggested I should be the Emperor of Pandahem. That is all a foolishness. I would sooner be the Grand Archbold of the Kroveres of Iztar."

"Yet this same Emperor of Vallia created the new emperor in Hamal, did he not?"

"Oh, aye, he did that. I was there."

"I would have you still as my hand in the world, Seg. And your new comrades here will prove fine krovere brothers. Even the Relt Caphlander, for the Order has need of a stylor."

"Agreed, my lady."

Milsi just stood, trembling finely in Seg's arms, listening to this talk of emperors . . .

"Also, Seg, I may tell you that the Emperor of Vallia has decided on your new kovnate. You are to be a High Kov. He would have you as an emperor like himself out of his comradeship." The mellow voice chimed golden gong notes. "Yet I think you do right to refuse for the moment."

"Look at Pandahem! They'd never accept an emperor. And as for this kingdom of Croxdrin, my lady Zena Iztar, I have decided."

"Excellent. Proceed."

"I shall do whatever my lady Milsi asks me to do."

The smile curved even more in that palely glowing face framed by the brown hair and the golden helmet.

"A very wise and sound decision, I assure you."

"But—!"

"The Kroveres of Iztar need you, Ver Seg. So do others of your blade comrades."

"Yes, and I can tell you why my old dom wants to make me the Emperor of Pandahem! The cunning old leem hunter—he's so fed up with his job as Emperor of Vallia and keeps trying to shovel it off onto his son Drak that he wants to let me have a taste of the same nonsense!''

Zena Iztar laughed. Her smile broadened and it seemed the twin suns of Scorpio flamed and blazed within the throne room there in jungle-fast Croxdrin.

''You are wrong, Ver Seg; but you do have a point. Now you must make your decision with the lady Milsi. There is much to do in the world, for Kregen never sleeps.''

And, like that, suddenly the golden radiance vanished and with a last faintly ringing: ''Remberee!'' vibrating on the air Zena Iztar departed.

Without hesitation Seg turned Milsi in his arms, kissed her lusciously and with immense passion and gusto, grabbed the crown, thrust it into her hands, lifted hands and crown and settled it on his head. Then he hopped down the steps and stood staring up at Milsi as the choirs all broke into song, the priests chanted, the music soared and the blue water dropped down plop after plop in the clepsydra.

When they were alone, the crowds still shouting and carousing in the streets outside and the torches flaring all over Nalvinlad and the wine flowing like the very river itself, she said severely: ''I understood a very great deal of what passed between you and the lady Zena Iztar. It seems, King Seg, that you have been keeping secrets from your wife.''

After he had kissed her a few times, he said: ''True.''

After she had kissed him some more times, she said: ''And what do you propose?''

"Do you think Mishti would happily go to Vallia?"

"I do not. She has grown apart from me since we arrived here. I do not blame Muryan for that. It is her youthfulness. She wants to be queen. It has gone to her—"

"And you?"

"I go with my husband."

He sat up, looking down on her glorious in the lamplight. "That's not good enough! I do what you want!"

She moved her hand against his chest.

"I do not like this jungly place, and that's the truth of it."

"You'll like Vallia, and Valka, and—"

"Will they like me?"

Seg laughed, but before he could gather her in his arms, she said: "I told you I understood. How could you be the Emperor of Pandahem? The island is made up of many countries. Yet—wait, wait, my love, let me finish. Yet you spoke of the Emperor of Vallia—and we all know what he did in Hamal. And you said he was your old dom. And he was the Bogandur, and he was—oh, Seg! Was he really?"

"As ever lived and breathed."

"Then I shall be happy in Vallia."

Then she reached up and kissed him on the nose, and said: "And even if the Emperor of Vallia was another Trylon Muryan, still I would be happy with you."

The next day they had to go about the city so that all the people might see them and cheer.

Presents were lavished, and Seg made a great point of acting with exquisite politeness to Kov

Llipton who accompanied them. They had reached
the royal jetty where the crowds waited, and everything was going splendidly. A slim paddler appeared from a tangle of craft and thrust vigorously
for the shore. Kov Llipton saw it, and his great
numim face broke into a delighted smile.

The schinkitree touched the jetty and a numim,
waving his wand of office high and shoving a little
Relt out of his way, leaped up onto the wooden
planking. He went straight into the incline, and
bellowed: "Pantor! Kov Llipton, I have urgent
information—"

"Stand up, Tyr Naghan Shore!"

Up leaped the numim, fierce, bubbling with his
news. Before Llipton could bellow out that the
queen and king stood before him, Naghan Shor
yelped: "I asked at the Vallian consulate, and they
confirm, my lord! This evil-smelling rascal, Seg
Segutorio, is indeed a kov of Vallia! I hope and
pray you have not sent him swimming—"

Seg near busted a gut laughing. Milsi put a hand
to her mouth. Even Kov Llipton in his numim way
let out a great guffaw of merriment.

Mind you, said Seg to himself, Llipton might
laugh now; but it had been touch and go. He'd
have sent Seg swimming, sure as the river rolled
to the sea, had events not turned out as they had.

A tremendous roar rose up from the crowds.
Everyone swiveled to stare down river and up—up
into the bright air.

They soared on, high and fast, swarm after
swarm of them. Fleet airboats, fast compact vollers,
enormous skyships, flying up the river in a silent
majestic procession. Many banners waved. Seg
didn't say a word; but the smile spread his mouth

right across his tanned face. Milsi clung to his arm.

Tyr Naghan Shore yelped as though a wersting had bitten his rump. His ferocious lion-man's face crumpled.

"May the Good Pandrite aid us now! Woe, woe! They are from Vallia, and they have come to chastise us for sending their kov Seg Segutorio the Horkandur a-swimming in the river!"

Seg rapped out: "Calm yourself, Tyr. I am Seg Segutorio. I live. They are my friends and we will welcome them in a seemly fashion."

Naghan Shore, the kov's messenger, gaped.

That enormous armada flew down, and hovered over the river, and everyone saw the snouts of the catapults and ballistae, the varters, those special varters of Vallia that could blow the crowds away in a twinkling. Of the many banners the union flag of Vallia dominated all.

A small voller swung out, circled, and landed where it seemed to the pilot the most important personages congregated.

From the flier stepped a lithe lissom man, hard-faced, bronzed, with a wild and reckless look about him. At his side stood a woman of great beauty, poised and regal. He wore war harness, she wore a laypom-colored gown of soft material and easy cut, yet she, too, carried weapons.

Seg smiled. People didn't know whether to stare at the new arrivals or gape at the armada above. The skyships were truly enormous, with decks serried one above the other, each with a long row of varter ports. Over the sides heads showed, staring down, hawk-faces, crowned with helmets, and the glitter of spear and sword, the deadly glint of arrowheads.

From a voller over the center of the river a pot fell. It blazed and spurted and spat fire. The hiss when it hit the water carried a message understood by all.

"Milsi," said Seg. "Here come the King and Queen of Hyrklana, Jaidur and Lildra. I see they brought company."

A hulking great fellow abaft the King of Hyrklana put a trumpet to his lips and blew. That brought instant silence. Into the quiet his stentorian bellow broke.

"We seek Kov Seg Segutorio! I tell you, on behalf of the King and Queen of Hyrklana, and of the Eleventh Fleet of the Vallian Air Service, that if you have harmed one hair of his head this entire miserable little city will be put to the flames!"

Seg stepped out and called: "Lahal Jaidur! Lahal Lildra!"

They ran to him, their hands extended.

"Uncle Seg!"

Then it was all an uproar, of shouting and laughter, of introductions, and of the promise of gargantuan feasts, with much eating and drinking, of dancing and singing. If there is one thing that any Kregan can do—bar a few of the more intractable of the races of diffs—it is have one hell of a good time.

"Yes, it was all good fortune," Jaidur told Seg in a reasonably quiet interlude. Milsi just hung onto Seg and wouldn't let him go. "This fellow came downriver and wanted to know if they should have your head off, or whatever—"

"Send a fellow swimming is the way of it here."

"Yes. Damned primitive. Anyway, a voller was there and old Strom Ornol—you remember him, Seg, whiskers as long as your arm and knows all the gods and goddesses in Hawkwa Country off by heart—spotted how important it was, as it was by Vox! The voller hared it back to the fleet. We're going to help Drak out, seems the idiots out of North Pandahem are trying another stupid invasion. So, here we are. And the quicker we're on our way home—although Hyrklana is my home now—" Here Jaidur in his reckless way gazed fondly on Lildra "—we can set about helping my big brother Drak."

"Ye-es—"

"You're taking this kingship thing here seriously?"

"Well, young Vax Neemusbane, you may have been a king longer than I have, for I've just begun; but I do take it seriously. Also, young man, there is a matter I must discuss with you that may make you sit up a trifle."

"Oh?"

Seg smiled. Give Jaidur a few more years yet before he was asked to join the Brotherhood of the Kroveres of Iztar. . . .

"All in good time."

"This is a splendid party you're having. Your coronation? Well, many congratulations. But Vallia needs us."

"In my own time, Jaidur. Give me but the one day?"

"Very well, Uncle Seg. Oh, and I hear that in this savage country all the queens are called Queen Mab and all the kings mean a great fat wo, a zero, empty of power and authority. I mean you no

disrespect, Seg, as you know full well, seeing that
you stand to me as my father. But you are King
Mabo, majister. King Mabo.''

"Aye, my lad, I am King Mabo. Also, the
kings meant nothing here beside the queens until
King Crox married Milsi's relation. The kings take
the name Mab and put it into the masculine gender.
Mabo. H'm.'' Here Seg wrinkled up his eyes and
pulled his lip and chuckled a trifle to himself,
softly. "Your father is not the only one to gather
up names to himself, it seems.''

During this day of grace, in which he must
make his decision, and in which he and the queen
must show themselves to the people of Nalvinlad,
Seg debated. In theory during the following weeks
they would travel up and down the length of the
Kazzchun River so that all their subjects might see
them.

He knew one fact for certain. If he went back to
Vallia he would take those of his comrades who
wished to come. He felt confident Diomb and
Bamba would leap at the chance. And as for
Malindi—Milsi had outfitted her with a wardrobe
that would not fit into a chest large enough to hold
six full grown men and demanding another six to
carry.

He cornered Kov Llipton when they stopped to
take a sup at the villa of Trylon Ortyg Lloton. He
gestured for Llipton's wife, the sumptuous Rahishta,
to remain. He spoke directly and hard, not soften-
ing his words.

"You dealt harshly with me, kov. Now I am
king I overlook that, for I perceive you were carrying out the duties entrusted to you as you saw fit. I

would have you less sudden and more inclined to
look into justice.''

"Aye, majistèr. But I sent to verify your tale.''

"You did, and that is why you still live and
hold your lands, estates, title and head. Yet I see
you delight in thus exercising a king's prerogatives
and power.''

Rahishta gasped. Llipton merely lowered his
head.

"Would you remain loyal to Queen Mab if she
left this country? Would you care for the lady
Mishti Mab if she remained?''

Kov Llipton lifted that massive lion head, and
stared full at Seg. He raised a hand. "I so swear
on the life of myself, my wife and my family, in
the sight of Numi-Hyrjiv the All-Glorious and of
Pandrite the All-Seeing.''

"So be it, Kov Llipton, and I give you joy of
your task—if the queen agrees.''

The hours dropped by, plop after plop in the
clepsydras.

"I shall not be sorry,'' said Milsi as they turned
back from a high balcony where the crowds below
cheered and shouted and sang. "I shall be down-
right glad to reach my bed this night.''

'' 'Tiredness is a sin,' '' quoted Seg.

When after due ceremony they were at last glori-
ously alone, Milsi sighed and said: "I know what
is in your mind, my heart. I believe that many
parts of Vallia are very similar to parts of Jholaix.''

"We grow fine grapes and make fine wine, but
not as fine as that of Jholaix. It is your decision,
and yours alone. You know my feelings—''

"And mine are just the same!''

"The first thing in the morning we shall tell Jaidur."

"Not too early!"

When they told Mishti next morning she tossed her head, declaring: "I am pleased! I am a grown woman, a princess, and I shall do what I do more freely. At least that cramph Muryan knew how to treat me as a queen."

"He told that archer to kill you, Mishti!"

"Yes, mother, he was a vengeful spirit. And where is that man? I will send him swimming, I swear—"

"He was just a Bowman of Loh," said Seg, "earning his hire."

Nag-so-Spangchin had disappeared, escaping clean away. With him went a bare score of his regiment of bowmen. Recalling the cast that struck the arrow from thin air, Seg felt the unease in him. He could be mistaken and, of course, no chance could possibly be taken in such a fraught moment— still and all, the doubt persisted. Everywhere people spoke of this miraculous shot, and marveled.

Everything was ready. Everything was prepared. Seg was not disappointed in his comrades. All would fly with him. He looked forward with pleasure to welcoming them to the ranks of the Kroveres of Iztar. And so the final moments came.

Skort and his Clawsangs held very firmly to stanchions and rails as the skyship lifted away. This flying was a novel and highly unsettling experience to them. Milsi remained cool and regal and altogether adorable, and Seg put his arm about her waist in sight of the crowds beneath and the uproar was prodigious.

"Remberee, majestrix! Remberee, majister!"

"We'll come back from time to time, Kov Llipton, unexpectedly. And we'll bring company." Seg nodded significantly skywards, where the swarms of airboats lifted, soaring up and away under the brilliance of the suns. "Remberee!"

Just before Mishti departed, she half-turned, and then swung back. Tears streamed down her cheeks. Impulsively, she flung herself forward and clasped her arms about Milsi.

"Oh, mother! I do love you, really! I do!"

"Yes, Mishti, of course you do, as I love you."

The little two-place voller took Mishti back to the care and protection of Kov Llipton. Seg felt very sure that that young lady would run a very tight ship down there along the Kazzchun River. Then he turned and looked up and forward.

Presently he and Milsi walked up into the prow of the skyship. Above them the flags flew. He was amused and touched to notice the splendid flag Milsi had made for him among the hosts of Vallian and Hyrklanian treshes.

"Well, my love?"

"And well to you, too."

"Jholaix and Vallia. Life is going to be very good."

"Life is going to be splendid!"

After a small silence, Seg said: "My lady Milsi, I wish to tell you how supremely happy you make me, how much I love and admire you, how deeply—"

She began to smile at his foolishness and then saw how deadly serious he was. She responded instantly.

"The same lightning bolt, Horkandur, my Jikai, Seg the Bowman."

And then King Jaidur of Hyrklana strolled up, cheerful to be on his way to his ancestral home. He saw the way the King and Queen of Croxdrin stood so closely, lost in each other. In his reckless way he called out:

"Done any good shooting lately, Uncle Seg?"

"Oh, a couple of reasonable casts. . . ."

**DAW**

Do you long for the great novels of high adventure such as Edgar Rice Burroughs and Otis Adelbert Kline used to write? You will find them again in these DAW novels, filled with wonder stories of strange worlds and perilous heroics in the grand old-fashioned way: